William Kenrick, McNamara Morgan, Porcupinus Pelagius

Remarkable Satires

The causidicade, The triumvirade, The porcupinade, The processionade, The 'piscopade, The scandalizade, and The pasquinade

William Kenrick, McNamara Morgan, Porcupinus Pelagius

Remarkable Satires
The causidicade, The triumvirade, The porcupinade, The processionade, The 'piscopade, The scandalizade, and The pasquinade

ISBN/EAN: 9783337409944

Printed in Europe, USA, Canada, Australia, Japan

Cover: Foto ©Andreas Hilbeck / pixelio.de

More available books at **www.hansebooks.com**

THE
TRIUMVIRADE:
OR,
BROAD-BOTTOMRY.
A Panegyri-Satiri-Serio-Comi-Dramatical
P O E M.

By PORCUPINUS PELAGIUS,
Author of the CAUSIDICADE.

Resurgit.	ANONY.
Ille ergo qui quondam——	VIRG.

THE

TRIUMVIRADE,

&c.

WHEN *Grantown* and *Bathen*, as Story records,
This Chief of the C-mm-ns and That of the L—ds,
Had broken the mighty *Leviathan*'s Pow'r,
After twenty long Years Oppoſition and more:
Quite routed his Partizans all to a Man,
While each cry'd, the De'il take the hindmoſt and ran:
The Sceptre ſubſided, and Sov'reign Command
For a Fortnight ſuſpended, at leaſt, thro' the Land.
The two heroic Chiefs ſat directing the Whole,
Yet mod'rate, howe'er, in the height of Controul.

In respectful Obedience to R-y-l Request,
As loth with Pr-r-g-tive much to contest,
And embroil all the Nation in Discord and Jarrs,
Give Room for *French* Agents to raise Civil Wars,
And practice upon us at home, while abroad
The proud common Foe on fair Liberty trod,
The Ballance of *Europe* o'erturn, and but deem us
Only worthy the Favour of proud *Poliphemus*.
These Considerations inducing, they err'd,
And fatally national Justice deferr'd,
Receiv'd into Mercy, not only, but Place,
'Mong others, the *Paym-ster*, *Scribe*, and the *M—e*,
Well said the *great Chief*, when he heard it, and true,
Who retains in his Bosom an Adder will rue,
So refus'd to concur in't, and greatly withdrew.

Prophetic he spoke, for e'er long the Ingrates
Resolv'd into Faction, and wrangling Debates:
Regardless of promis'd Submission in Station,
Their precarious Condition, and late Situation;
Some dreading the Axe, and some others the String,
Distress'd both th' Affairs of the S—te and the K——g.
For whate'er Proposal by *Grantown* was made,
For the Good of the Nation in War and in Trade,
Was strongly oppos'd, tho' oppos'd long in vain,
As his Sov'r—n did e'er the Opposition restrain:

'Till

'Till the Statefman, indignant, to find 'em perfift,
And revolving the Confequence deep in his Breaft;
How the Nation muft fuffer, himfelf be too vex'd,
And his Sov'r—n by diff'rent crofs Counfels perplex'd:
With true Patriot Care, as good *Sommers*, fam'd Lord,
Did honeftly erft deal with *W—ll—m* the Third,
He fincerely advis'd, for his Int'reft 'twas beft,
To let him withdraw, for a while at the leaft.
The Mon—ch, reluctant, complied with th' Advice,
As he hardly could e'er find a Statefman like *This*.
Prodigious his Talents and form'd for the Helm,
E'er ftudious to unite both the K—g and the R—lm,
An Enemy always profefs'd againft *France*,
Their Faith fo perfidious, and vain Complaifance.

Refigning, he gratified all their Defires,
Depriv'd of his Counfel, the K—g follow'd theirs;
Confufion enfu'd, wild Debate and Uproar,
Betwixt thofe who'd come *in*, and thofe *in* before:
Many Schemes were invented, but none could fucceed,
And many were call'd, tho' but few wou'd concede.
However *Broadbottymry* gain'd unawares,
That Monfter which ruin'd great *W—ll—m*'s Affairs;
Diftracted his Councils, obftructed his Meafures,
And crampt, both at home and abroad, all his Meafures,

As

As a firm Coalition could never yet be,
Since the *Whig* and *the Tory* could never agree;
And, if Right I the Figure of Prophecy cast,
Their future Behaviour you'll find like the past;
Mistrustful and jealous, they'll stir up Debate,
And, to cross one another, will ruin the S—te.

But what mostly perplex'd 'em (as *Præses*, the sage,
With caution, declin'd to expose his old Age
To Contest and Faction) was, who shou'd be PRIME,
'Till they wisely agreed to confer it on him,
Whose Head, upon Measure, should longest be found,
But the Mischief on't was, they were all short and round.
Of equal Dimensions, than deep rather shallow,
So that neither could cast a Reproach on his Fellow.
Since therefore amongst them, it could not be said,
There was fit for the Service one single good Head,
They resolv'd still more wisely, to try if they cou'd,
By joining their Heads, the Deficience make good.
In the Counsel of many there is Safety we count,
And a Group of *short* Heads to one *Long* may amount.

To vacate and fill up the Places, of those
Whom they had, in their Wisdom, proscrib'd as their Foes,

They

They debated with Caution and Care, as they knew
From the Error of *Grantown* their Politics true:
But first importun'd, with unanimous Voice,
Since the Station of PRIME met not *Præses*'s Choice,
He'd vouchsafe, at the least, to assist with his Care,
And, resuming th' old Office, relinquish the *Chair*.
Tho' a Post of great Honour, yet well might be fill'd,
By one in th' Affairs of the Public less skill'd.
" Your Ability call you to serve, quo' his *Gr—ce*,
" Where Experience is wanted, to wit, your old Place.
" None can abler the long-headed *Grantown* succeed,
" And only your Wisdom can his supercede."
His L-rdship with Honour and Business quite cloy'd,
Wou'd fain have remain'd in the Place he enjoy'd.
Arriv'd as it were, safe in Port from the Main,
Was loth to launch out into Hurry again;
But howe'er, as with Faction he never took Part,
But had always his K—g and his Country at Heart;
In Honour of these, he vouchsaf'd to resume,
But look'd with Regret on the Post he came from.

Th' Assembly broke up and adjourn'd for a Time,
And whisper'd about, that whoever wou'd trim
And come to their Scheme, on the ***Broadbottom*** Plan,
Shou'd be wellcome, and all be preferr'd to a Man:

Provided

Provided they would not obſtruct the Supply,
And join in their Meaſures great *John* to decry.
The Deſign took Effect, lo! the Creatures all cringe,
By Avarice prompted and Hopes of Revenge,
In the Sun-ſhine of Promiſe they wantonly baſk'd,
And implicitly gave into all that was aſk'd;
They paſs'd the S-pp-ly, without one ſingle Nay,
And ſo loyal were all the good C-mm-ns that Day,
That had but ſome M—ber the Motion promoted,
They'd as Uſeleſs that poor Monoſillable voted.
Nay the Sons of old *Jacob* themſelves, it is ſaid,
Were ſo pleas'd with the Hopes of again making Head,
That they wrote to their Party, awhile to ſuſpend
Putting Bumpers about to their old *Roman* Friend,
Until further Orders how each ſhould comport,
And that *W—tk—n* had once been again at the C——.

Tho' the two virtuous H—ſes obediently did
Whatever our mighty *Triumvirate* bid;
Yet Matters went on very ill at St. *J——s*
For his old faithful Servant the *Great one* exclaims.
Return me my Friend, my great Stateſman, quo' he,
Who can equal his Skill? not together you Three.
Scribonius, perhaps, you'll aver you can write,
Suppoſe it be granted——ſay who will indite?

'Tis

'Tis not the prompt Hand, nor the Mind will suffice,
'Tis the Head that can counsel alone and devise.
I'll allow you may head, on Occasion, a Mob,
And fight, like old *Ziska* himself, with a Club;
Drive *Tories* and *Ormonites* all down before ye,
And acquire with proud *Bell* of the Post-Office Glory.
But say; can you stem the proud *Gaul* and *Bavar*,
And sustain, 'gainst the *P—ssian* perfidious, the War?
No, no, as but fit for domestic Affairs,
Little Matters left *Grantown* alone to your Cares.
Mind therefore your Province, suppress the Sheep-Stealers,
* Street-Robbers and Gamblers, and Journeymen Taylors.

You *Thesaurus*, may boast your great Skill in Account
And the Manage of Payments: but when you have don't,
Can you fill up the Coffers of St—e with Supply,
Or, in Treaty, with foreign Ambassadors vie?
Tho' you did very well, when old *Bobb* held the Wand,
And acted with Diligence under Command;
Yet to act and to think are quite diff'rent, I deem,
Ways and Means are not easy, tho' *Scrope*'s in the Scheme.

C And

* Vid. Several late Gazettes.

And you with your Gold-tufted Gown and the M——,
Your Tragedy Wig, and your Madam-like Face,
Preceded in Pomp by a Croud of mean Fellows,
Which you took from the Dirt, like **, as they tell us;
From the proud aukward Bumpkin who carries the P—ſe,
To that ſimple young Fellow, who hangs at your A—.
Do you think that Bench-Learning and Preſident Prate
Can ſufficiently qualify Men for the S—te?
Go, withdraw to your Office, and keep in that Sphere,
Or, perhaps, you may pay for your Forwardneſs dear.
Remember the Fate of your Patron; when he,
Neglecting his Poſt, fain a Stateſman wou'd be.
His Vices and Views and his ill-gotten Store,
His defrauding of Orphans and grinding the Poor,
Had paſt unexamin'd, and Perquiſites deem'd,
Had he kept to his *Laſte* and ne'er aim'd to have climb'd.
Have you carried your Cup then ſo even d'ye think,
As ne'er to have ſpill'd one Drop of good Drink?
If ſo: Yet remember that mine are the S—ls,
Lo! *R—d—r* makes Intereſt, and ready is *W—s*.

The *Triumvirate* yet, notwithſtanding this Check,
Reſolv'd to go on and digeſt the *Rump Steak*.
What tho' at the Threſhold a little, they tript?
Pray why ſhou'd they fear? they're too big to be whipt.

What

What tho' they're forsook by their *K—g* and by Heav'n,
Recourse to the Devil may make Matters even.
A good Scripture Text, for the Purpose, they quoted,
I think it was somewhere in *Samuel* noted;
How without the Assistance of Lightning and Thunder,
As now does our *Faustus*, the good Witch of *Endor*,
Did without the least Noise, save alone her own Squall,
Raise the Prophet, or Devil, or both up to *Saul*.

But a-pox on the Spoak that's got into the Wheel;
Not one single Conj'rer to talk with the De'il,
Can they find in their Party; no, not even one!
For the Conjurers all are engag'd with great *John*.
Well-a-day and a-lack! must the Project be foil'd,
And their Porridge, for want of a Conjurer, spoil'd?
What then's to be done? all their Counsels run various,
'Till united at last by the great *C-nc-ll-rius*.

A Conjurer's Sphere, *under Favour I speak it*,
I'n't so difficult sure, but we may undertake it.
With humble Submission, quo' he, my Compeers
We can make up, among us, a Conjurer's Geers.
Lo! I've a long Robe, as all Conjurers have,
And your *Honour* a Wand, and your *G—ce* can engrave

Black illegible Characters, ſcratch'd like your Title,
And all muſt allow you can ſcribble a little.
Behold! then a Conjurer's Enſigns compleat?
And now for a Head to go thro' with the Feat.
If better than one, are two Heads, you'll allow
That three muſt of Courſe be yet better than two.
Join we then *Pericrania*, ſo ſep'rately fam'd,
And if we don't conjure, by G—d I'll be damn'd.
Pleaſe God! we ſhall ſoon, with th' Aſſiſtance of theſe,
Raiſe the Devil in *propria Perſona* with Eaſe.
So a Circle he ſtruck with the Wand on the Floor,
And thus he incanted Hell's Sovereign Pow'r.
" Oh! Thou who preſid'ſt o'er the Caverns below,
" Where Nitre and Brimſtone in livid Flames glow;
" Where Stateſmen, Phyſicians, and Lawyers abide,
" And Placemen for voting, and Biſhops beſide!
" Sole Diſpoſer of Riches, Preferment and Gain,
" And Garters and Honours and Pleaſure and Pain.
" By whom as *Triumvirates*, here we command,
" And hold theſe *Inſigna*; *M—e*, *S—ls*, and the *W—d*;
" Attend in this perilous Time and aſſiſt,
" In forming a ſolid, good *Broadbottom* Liſt."

Not long had they pray'd, as the courteous poor Devil,
Is to Votaries ever obliging and civil;

Keeps

Keeps none in Sufpence, like his *Honour* or *Grace*,
When they cringe at the Levy for Penfion or Place.
Strait a Rumbling was hear'd and the Floor open'd wide,
Like the Stage in the Playhoufe for Ghofts in to glide.
The *Triumvirates* trembling, were fhock'd at the Sight!
All their Hair ftood an end! —— and up popp'd a Sprite.
A Coronet Ducal furrounded his Head,
On a Wand he fupported a Body well fed;
Thefaurus look'd pale and conceiv'd that fome L—d
Wou'd engrofs to himfelf all the Tr—f—y Board:
But was foon undeceiv'd, fince the grave folemn *Thing*,
Bounc'd, dropping the Wand, to the *Chair* with a
   Fling.
Lo! it faid, or at leaft the *Thing* feem'd to have faid:
" The Decree of the Power, to whom you have pray'd,
" Who lives in the Country at K—— unbelov'd,
" Yet by truckling at C——t has been long there ap-
   prov'd:
" Who among Country Neighbours erects up a Port,
" Yet can ftoop to the *C—tefs*'s Servants at C——t,
" Is kick'd, from a Poft of more Profit, up Stairs,
" Supremely to nodd in the *Chair* of all Chairs."

Then follow'd a Coronet equal in Size,
Of equal Importance and equally wife;

With

With unducal Submiſſion he took up the Wand,
Bow'd low and march'd on with the Bawble in Hand.
Took his Place next the Firſt, and then ſaid, "my
"good Friends,
"Your Servant concurs in your politick Ends.
"Juſt arriv'd from my Government o'er the poor *Bog*,
"Where I reign'd, without Pow'r, like a kind of King
"*Logg*;
"E'en without the poor Privilege, hardly to give
"A Place in my Kitchen to any alive.
"In minuteſt Affairs, I was tied to Account
"With Leviathan *Bobb*; mighty Lord Paramount!
"That thus was the Caſe, you will promptly agree,
"As yourſelves were accountable alſo, like me;
"Old *Satan* rejoices and greets you all Three.

Next appear'd in an Inſtant direct thro'. the Door,
And not from the De'il thro' the Hole in the Floor,
A Form pretty much on the ſhort and rotund,
By many much prais'd, and by others much d—nn'd.
On his Right appear'd Wit, very ſprightly and gay;
Good Senſe on his Left ſhone as bright as the Day.
In the Converſe of theſe he alternately ſhone,
And at laſt found the Secret to join them in one.
Sound Wiſdom and Judgment attended aloof,
And waited his Nodding ſome little Way off.

But

But ſeldom of either of theſe he made Uſe,
Except now and then in Debate at the *H-uſe.*
Behind him the Muſes ſwept all in a Train,
Illumin'd his Mind and intun'd his ſoft Vein.
While Glory diſplay'd round his Head in a Blaze,
And Honour broke forth on his Boſom in Rays.
With ev'ry great Quality happily bleſt,
Like th' affable *P—g—tt*, great Genius! deceaſt.
Ah! *P—g—tt*, by Arts and the Sciences mourn'd,
Deplor'd by the Muſes he lov'd and the Learn'd:
Leſs noble by Birth than by Talents well known,
And, perhaps, by *Phil Nobilis* equall'd alone.
Diſdainfully coy, look'd our Wit on the *Three*,
And ſaid, prithee *Meſſieurs*, your Pleaſure with me?
'Tis to give you whatever you pleaſe, anſwered They,
So you quit for the State your great Paſſion for ——
In the one you excel and go thro' without Trouble.
In to'ther you labour to ſhew you're a Bubble.
" As the *Legacy* left (replied he) is near gone,
" A Riſque of refunding I hardly can run;
" 'Twas meant to diſtreſs, whom the Donor call'd
" K———s,
" But to fall in with F——s me at Liberty leaves.
" If to ſerve I vouchſafe, it's for State and Parade,
" Not for Lucre and Gain as of late was your Trade.

 " Viceroy

" Viceroy over *Bogland*, with plentiful Pow'rs,
" And subject alone to my *K—g*'s, and not yours,
" With Disposal of Place, alone is my Choice,
" And that Trade and Land-Interest be made to re-
" joice."
Be it so, quo' the *Three*, so you think not too much
To hasten to *H-ll-nd* to bring in the *D—ch*.

Soon after him rises the Shade of old *G*——
" I'm doom'd to the Office, quo' he, I'd before.
" 'Tis true I resign'd, but it was in a Pet,
" The rash foolish Action I still do regret.
" Yon *Cestrian* must instantly quit and make room,
" Lo! *H-n-v-r G——r*, now returns to his Home,
" With a D—ke in his Hand, fine and gay like a
" Plume."

He hardly had finish'd, e're *Cestrius* came in,
His Countenance comely and placid his Mien,
Tho' sullied a little, by nightly Debauch,
Bad Hours, and bad Comp'ny, and drinking too much;
An Aversion t'inspect his domestic Affairs,
While yet for the Public's remark'd for his Cares.
E'er bounteously lib'ral, in giving away,
But confoundedly slow or to thrive or to P——.

Ne-

Neglectful th' *Insigna* of Office he held,
And with Gentleneſs on his Competitor ſmil'd.
G—r ſmuſh'd them away, and, with ſatisfied Looks,
Exultingly plac'd himſelf 'twixt the two *D—s*.
While *Ceſtrius* declar'd " I reſign them with Eaſe,
" Since the Clerks ſink the Perquiſites all and the Fees:
" And the more, as I find, 'tis his M-j--y's Pleaſure
" T' appoint me in *Bogland*, VICE o'er his Treaſure.
" As he whoſe Oeconomy's bad o'er his own,
" May manage, by Paradox, beſt for the C——n,
" Quo' NIXON, our Families *ſeer* on Record;
" And ſacred is *Nixon*'s prophetical Word.
" As Both Fate and my Sov'reign declare on my Side,
" I inſiſt on Compliance, in ſpite of your Pride."
To the *K—g*, anſwer'd they, we're Obedient and Civil,
Tho' here we acknowledge no Pow'r but the D—l.

Next bolts up a Coronet, dapper and ſhort,
'Twas Ducal, with *Tory* inſcrib'd on his Heart.
Spite of former Engagements, Reſolves and great Coſt,
He comes from the Devil to accept of a Poſt.
" Tho' once, quo' the Shade, (as indeed 'twas no more)
" In the Days of my Folly, ſometime, heretofore,
" At the gay, Duke of *M—lb—h*, diſdainful, I laught,
" For ſuffering himſelf to be taken by Craft:

" Yet now I'm convinc'd, there are few can resist,
" The Charms of C—t Favour, so *properly* prest.
" Notwithstanding my vast and unbounded Estate,
" Which well with Revenues of Princes may mate,
" A resistless Propension impels me to crouch
" At C—t for a Post, and some Thousands to touch.
" As, howe'er, to a Point, it is known I am stub-
" born,
" You have heard of my naval Affairs down at *W*——
" Cross that vast Sea-Canal, I've successfully sail'd,
" And yet was I never once Shipwreck'd or fail'd.
" The Structure of Shipping I well understand,
" And how to give Orders to sail———o'er the Land.
" Oft I've been in great Battles, altho' but in Mock,
" And bravely bore up 'gainst the Danger and Shock;
" The huge double E—l, who sits as first L——d,
" And leads all the rest by the Nose at the B——d.
" Must yield in Experience to me, all allow,
" As a *D*—— is more skill'd than an E—l you know;
" Notwithstanding the two Chrystal Wheels, which in-
" close,
" With monstrous Circumf'rence, the Tip of his Nose;
" And that on Twelfth Night, by his *Legerdemain*,
" He may strip us new C——tiers perhaps, of our
" Gain.

Well

Well ken we your Meaning (quo' the THREE) my Lord
D——,
A *Grantonite* he! and contemns our Rebuke.
He, and all his Aſſociates, we'll ſoon ſet aſide,
Save one, who ſhall ſtand new C-m-ſſi—rs to guide.
Your Gr— ſhall ſit Chief, and a Seaman the laſt,
With four noble L—ds, and a Counſellor vaſt!
He approving withdrew, bowing low as he paſt.

The reſt of the B—d, in a Group did advance,
Up aloft thro' the Chaſm, as tho' 'twere at once.
One put up as Grandſon to *Neptune* his Claim,
Whoſe Knowledge deriv'd down to him with the Name:
And 'tis hard, if a noble Deſcendant ſhould fail
In his Anceſtors Art, of the Rudder and Sail.
Another ſupported his Title, as he
Had ſail'd once to *M—yland* over the Sea.
What tho' he's built Ships, which the Winds can ne'er
move,
Yet that is no Reaſon but he may improve.
A *Fourth* for a Seat at the B—d muſt prevail,
By *Female* Pretenſions, as ſome ſay, *in Tail*.
A *Fifth* urg'd moſt ſtrongly he'd been in there before,
And was Son to a *D*——, who was Son of a ——.
The *Sixth*, tho' he owned he knew little of Tar,
Yet ſaid, he cou'd plead for the B—d at the Bar;

For the reſt he referred them to *C-bb-m*, 'not loth
To clench, on Occaſion, his Tale with an Oath.
The *Seventh*'s Pretenſions were ample and ſtrong;
He had tied up the Univerſe round in a Thong.
What tho' his whole Squadron of Ships he had loſt,
Save one he brought, foundering, home to our Coaſt.
Yet he did his own Bus'neſs, you'll ſay, very well;
Yea, and that at the Nation's Expence, I can tell.

They hardly had taken their Places around,
But *Aron Dell* flounc'd thro' the Hole in the Ground;
With *Parvulus Tonus* cloſe following in haſte,
As tho' not well pleas'd that he mounted up laſt.
But, bleſs me! how lank, how meagre, and ſtrait!
Run up, like bad Weeds, to a wonderful Height.
Juſt like *Little Tony*'s long Portrait in Print!
Soon the Firſt, as the Maſter, was known of the *M——t*;
A kind of a Steward to Turnpikes e'er that,
Well plaid he his Cards 'mong the great ones of State;
And yet not ſo wond'rouſly well, as he chanc'd
To get by the Dint of mere Wedlock advanc'd.
Know you not, who 'twas married the *one* and who *t'other*,
And who in the Law, is by Conſequence, Brother?

As 'tis ſaid, that by Kiſſing goes Favour at C——t,
They're diſtinguiſh'd of Courſe, who with Siſters conſort.
Thus Pentateuc *A-ron*, with *M-ſes* of old,
Shar'd, as Brother in Law, both in Places and Gold.
Quo' *Tonus*, for he cou'd beſt ſpeak as a Poet,
And that he's no bad one our fair ones allow it.
" Lo! before you a Brace of good T—ſ—y Lords,
" For ſo it is written below in Records.
" In the room of old *G—bſ—u* and *C—pt—n* we come,
" Who' beneath your *Triumvirate* Pleaſure ſuccumb.
" A Pair of known *Grantonites*." Be't ſo, quo' the *Three*,
We all very chearfully ſign the Decree.

Who happily had to Paternals of late,
Got added a lucrative Name and Eſtate.
Don Gorgo Bubb Dodo, creeping up, on all Fours,
With Care and with Caution the Trap-Hole explores.
" A Poet, quo' he, long diſtinguiſh'd by Fame,
" And known by all critical Judges, I am.
" The Praiſes of many I've ſung heretofore,
" And among them, pox on't, of Sir *Bob* in his " Pow'r.
" Very great is the Largeſs I'd give to ſuppreſs
" Thoſe Verſes, of which I'm aſham'd I confeſs.

" They're flat in my Teeth contradicting each Word,
" In my Speeches made since, as those Speeches record.
" To praise first in Verse, then abuse him in Prose,
" Does rather my own, than his Weakness expose.
" Great *Temple* did wisely to burn what he'd writ
" In *Arlington*'s Praise, when he found he was bit.
" But a Candidate now I appear to your G—e,
" And both your Compeers, for the Tr—s—r's Place.
" The *Bar'net* that I may get in must resign,
" Old *Nick* has declar'd in the Shades it is mine,"
And so do we here (quo' the Three) make it thine.

The high-favour'd *Wallo*, blind Fortune's bright Son,
Who forever commem'rates the Year *Twenty-one*.
Great Patron in *Broadbottom* Writing's Behalf,
By Bum-Flogger *G-th—y*, and Gazetteer *R——ph*,
Succeeds in the Hole, and as Candidate stands,
For the *C—ff—r*'s Place 'gainst the Patrio Lord ——.
Said, the Council infernal, declar'd it was his,
With the Perquisites all and the Poundage and Fees.
" Tho', quo' he, it requires neither Talents nor Skill,
" And that even Dunces the Station may fill;
" As 'tis plain, if we measure, by Deputy *O——d*,
" Who must pack up his Awls, and march off with
" his Lord.

" Yet

" Yet I, by Misfortune and Accident, am
" Better qualified for it than all you can name.
" The K—g's Civil List, as of late stands the Case,
" You know's in Arrear, about two Years space.
" The Houshold grow clam'rous for Pay and uneasy,
" And even the Judges, for Salary, tease ye.
" This Noise, and this Clamour can ne'er reach my
" Ear,
" Ti'n't proper the *C-ff—r* always should hear."
Quo' the *Triumvirs* right, your Pretensions are clear.

Lo! ascends from the Cavity, loud in a Storm,
A truly original *Broadbottom* Form.
A Broadbottom Substance all over, I vow,
Heads, Shoulders, and Arms, and, as all will allow
In th'Extent of the Word, *Broadbottom'd* below.
'Twas thence, first the Term had the Honour to come,
Broadbottomry sprung from our Baronet's Bum:
A distinguishing Characteristic for Mirth,
O! *ye Knights of the Bum*, kiss the Place of your Birth.
" I'm come, quo' the Bulk, up from *Tartarus* here,
" To acquaint the *Triumvirate* how they must steer.
" The De'il gives his Service, his Love, and all that,
" And wishes a joyful new Year to the State.

" In

" In Council ſits round him the *Jacobite* Clan,
" From the firſt of K— *J——es* to the laſt of Queen
" *A—*.
" There, after Debate, 'tis decreed for your Safety,
" ('Gainſt the *Grantonites* other Relief is not left ye)
" To take in the T—ys, to Favour and Grace,
" And that I be *immediately* put into Place,
" With three or four more; and ſo on, by Degrees,
" 'Till to Power and Council Friend *W—tk—n* you
" ſqueeze.
" But as you may think me, perhaps, ſuch a Fool,
" To tell my own Party ſome Tales out of School,
" I aſk not, at preſent, a Poſt in the State,
" Tho' a Lord at the B—d I was nam'd for of late
" I cou'd like very well; but clear as the Amber
" Is my Right to preſide o'er the Caſh *in the Chamber*.
" Nor has *Somebody* Cauſe at my Sight to be ſcar'd,
" As once in the Gardens at *Richmond* it far'd.
" Far be it from me to have acted *ſo* baſe,
" I'm the quieteſt *Thing* in the World —— in a Place."
E'er bleſt (quo' the *Three*) be Hell's great anointed.
Who ſuch great Politicians has wiſely appointed!
And that our Intrigues he eſpouſes ſo hearty,
To ſcreen us from Long-headed *John* and his Party.
Whom, at Court, and in Country, the People eſteem
As one who can puzzle the De'il at a Scheme.

But,

But, Heaven be prais'd, the good Devil we find,
Is too many for *John* when supported by *H—de.*
He crouch'd most respectfully low, as well pleas'd
To be thus by the mighty *Triumvirate* prais'd.

Lord *Hob* over heard, as he near was at hand,
And most righteously rose to oppose the Demand.
" Since it's come to that pass (quo' he) that you take-
" up,
" Against all the *pure ones*, with th' old Sons of *Jacob*,
" To the Mob I will call, like my Sire (holy Lubbard)
" *You, who stand by Ch---t J-s-s, cry* H--B--T *an*
" H--B--T!
" But let him, howe'er have the Place, you are rapt-in,
" Provided that I be made Battle-Ax Captain.
" Each Gentleman P-ns--ner's Place I can sell
" For Eight Hundred Pounds——I the Diff'rence can
" tell."
When suddenly up from the Hole came a Groan
As tho' 'twas L—d *B——st.* " In Spite I'm undone,
" Of the R-y-al Command;" yet appear'd not his
Ghost
So that ev'ry one gave him quite over for lost.

A loud Halloo follow'd, as tho' 'twou'd deprive ye,
Of your Ears and your hearing of Tontara, Teivy.

Hoa! *Ringwood* and *Jowler* and *Ranter* and *Nox*,
As if that old *Nick* was in Chace of a Fox.
Not ſo: but the new common-Hunt of the C—t,
Was ſtealing from *J-n-ſ-n* all his Support;
Hallooing the B--k Hounds away from his Care,
And leave in their Room but a Rope and Deſpair.
Oh Fie! that a P--r, in whom Learning abounds,
Should preſide over the Kennel, and run with the Hounds.

Will Prattle roſe next, deriv'd from th' old *Boa'ſon*,
(Who an *Indian* did firſt of a Diamond cozen;
Next the Factory plunder'd and afterwards ran)
With his Limbs very weak and his Face very wan.
He ſaid, tho' for Places he did not much care,
Yet, if he got well, he'd be Clerk of the War,
So he found it conſiſtent to accept of a Place,
With the large Patriot Legacy left by her G—ce.
And that they conſented to make Matters even,
By reducing to *Three* the odd Number of *Seven*:
For who cou'd a Prattler more aptly ſucceed
Than he, who can prattle ſo well in his Stead?
Whereupon cry'd the Oeconomiſt *Redſtring*, if ſo,
I or to the *Marſhal* or *Warden* muſt go.

Then the famous *Convention* Negociator, *K*—,
A ſhopkeeping Ald-rm-n's Son down at *Lynn*;

Erſt

Erſt a *Bobbite*, but ſince, a true *P—lh—ite* grown,
(For the *Bobbs* and *Pells*, now 'tis ſaid, are not one,)
Rears up thro' the Gap, in original Dung,
Kicking Paym—r *H—p—r* before him along.
" This Man, who, as Lawyer, a R-gue is of courſe,
" And yet, as a *S—t C-m—ee*-man, worſe;"
(Quo' the DON,) " as Deſerter I'm order'd to chaſe,
" With a few decent Kicks, from his ill-gotten Place:
" And ſo to ſucceed him myſelf; as anon
" I muſt vacate my Place, to make Room for *Sir* J—N.
" That Place, which with M—ber for *W—ſt—w*, I
" got,
" At th' Expence of the Nation, to make up a V-te,
" And for wiſely *conventioning* Diff'rences up;
" Tho' the *Grantonites* ſaid I deſerv'd but a Rope."

The Knight —— no, the Barr'net, of Britiſh Race
reckon'd,
That expell'd the old *Flemings* of HENRY the Second,
Like the De'il his old Friend, when he follow'd the Bar,
Is near when he's nam'd, or at leaſt is not far.
Yet diff'ring in all other Qualities wide,
For his Sire was a *Methodiſt* Saint *without* Pride.
Both himſelf and *Jack P—t*, (I mean *P—t* the rich
They're ſo many, one hardly can tell, which is which)

Shot lovingly up from the Depth of the Hole
Pinn'd together like Poppets, by Cheek and by Jowl,
Declar'd, howe'er large their Poſſeſſions and clear,
They cou'd yet, thro' Government's *Thouſand a Year*,
Diſtinguiſh Things clearer: and therefore were made,
On the *Broadbottom* Footing, C-mm-ſſ—rs of Trade.

Soon after ſteps up to the Floor, with a Strut
A Dueliſt, known by the Name of *Will Smutt*.
In Purſuit of a Creature, ycleapt a Buffoon!
Good Sirs! how it chatter'd, and jok'd on a Pun!
But howe'er that may be; with a brandiſhing Sword
Our Hero had like thro' its Guts to have bor'd;
E'er well from ſupporting its Breeches it cou'd,
Its Hands diſengage in Defence of its Bloud.
Will reverendly bow'd when he ſaw the great *Three*
And ſaid, a good Place is appointed for me.
Friend *Satan* this Moment has giv'n me the Hint
I'm call'd to ſucceed to the Chief of the *M—t*.

After ſhort Intermiſſion, a North Country Sprite,
Starts up in a Rage, from the Dark into Sight.
Th' ilk Devil, quo' he, curſe o' G—d on his Soll,
Ha nae notic'd one *Scot* for a Place on his Scroll.
Iſe therefore appeal to you Three 'gainſt his Spleen,
And inſiſt to be ſome way or other let in;

As

As my Merit is proven ye can nae refuse,
Or I'll vote with my Conscience next Time in the Hoose.
Ken you nae I'm a Dealer in Speech-making Words?
And can whiten and black as Occasion affords.
This Neglect of the *Scots* is a Breach of Union,
As may'nt be soon cur'd in my humble Opinion:
Ise therefore with gude lang-tail'd Speeches will brave ye,
An you don't put me soon at the Board of the N—y.
Quo' the Triumvirs, take it, so among us we have ye,
* * * * * * * * * * * * * * *
* * * * * * * * * * * * * *Desunt multa*

E'er the Candidates hardly were put in their Traces,
And reciprocal Compliments made on their Places.
A Crack of loud Thunder burst over the Room,
As tho' that in Earnest the Devil was come.
Howe'er 'twas not so: and yet almost as bad,
Our *Triumvirs* ne'er a worse Sight cou'd have had,
For the Ceiling, lo! opens, and *Grantown* drops down,
With a Smile on his Countenance, mixt with a Frown;
A triple crown'd Hero supported his Right,
On the Left shone *Britannia*, triumphantly bright.

Our

Our *Triumvirs* ſcar'd, march'd off in great Haſte,
Diſmounted, *unſtaff'd*, *unſeal'd*, and *unmac'd*,
While *Grantown* turn'd out all the reſt and diſplac'd;
Reſtor'd to his K—g the Pre——ve Sword,
And ſecur'd to the People their *ancient Record*;
Replac'd all his Friends, and ſtood firm like a Tow'r,
Defending *Britannia* from abſolute Pow'r,
In Honour, in Glory, in Peace and in Store.

THE

THE
PORCUPINADE,
A very POETICAL
P O E M.

To which is prefixed,

A COPY of *ſmooth* commendatory RHYMES to the AUTHOR,

FROM

PORCUPINUS PELAGIUS,
Author of the TRIUMVIRADE.

Aut inſanit homo, aut verſus facit.	HOR.
Thus each ſhould down with all he thinks;	PRIOR.
And all he thinks not.	ANON.

By *QUIDNUNCCIUS PROFUNDUS.*

THE

ROUPINADE:

A very POETICAL

POEM.

To which is prefixed,

[illegible] commendatory

HYMN [illegible],

FROM

CUPINUS PELAGIUS,

[illegible]

[illegible]

TO THE

AUTHOR,

On his Unanſwerable

POEM.

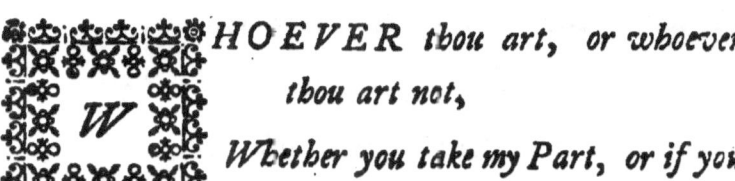

WHOEVER thou art, or whoever thou art not,
Whether you take my Part, or if you take my Part not,
I care not five Farthings; nay, without a Fee
That I'm juſt to your Merit, you'll ſpeedily ſee.

Your Lays are ſo highly ſublime and orac'lous,
While all from the Fetters of Rhyme you unſhackle us,
That, beneath your Ænigmas, but give me your Hand down,
Nought's meant againſt G——le, I'll bring you to Grantown:
He admires your fine Poets, a noted Mæcenas,
When he meets, Sir, like yours, with a * *ſingular Genius:*
And reaſons *ſo* plainly *the Nation may ſee,*
To be potent and great, at the leaſt they muſt be,
With firm Reſolution, and perfect Accord,
As virtuous, and ſober, and kind as—my Lord.
'Tis late in the Wane of the Moon you may ſay,
If you are a Swiſs *Poet, enlighten'd by Pay:*
But remark a prophetic and politic Pen,
Strange Things have occurr'd, and may happen agen.

By

* *Query*, whether *Pelagius* intended this, and indeed the whole, ſeriouſly or ironically?

By your Stile you ſhould be ſome aſpiring young Lad;
Fourſcore's an old Laureat—*and Odes muſt be bad:*
There's Sack in the Caſe, I might ſay in the Butt;
More of that tête à tête—*now a freſh Caſe to put.*
Suppoſe, while Affairs are removing and moving,
For our Splendour hereafter, and preſent improving,
We commute, change and barter, ſay, ſpeak and rehearſe;
I, political Lectures; you, Lectures in Verſe:
Whence we both may adorn the Republick of Letters;
And—a Word in your Ear—be of uſe to our Betters.
Your Method entirely your own I eſteem,
And your Meaning lies deep; tho' to ſome it may ſeem
Neither this, that, nor t'other, Rhyme, Reaſon, nor Law,
But a File for thoſe Serpents the Critics to gnaw.
You'll obſerve by my Plan, in high Secrets I'm deep;
And what Secrets you have I'll be ſworn you can keep.

Then as to my Writings, 'tis plain, they must take well

From the many Editions, as well as the Sequel.

*'Tis needless to add—let * one Int'rest combine us ,*

PELAGIUS *won't rhyme, but your Pig*

PORCUPINUS.

* *Query*, If the learned *Porcupinus* means by this, that we should divide the contingent Reversion of the Laurel, and become Twin-Laureats, as *Beaumont* and *Fletcher* were Twin-Playwrights. This may not be improbable, if we consider, that the modern Poets are not more remarkable for their Candour and Disinterestedness than the Physicians. It seems at least, that he has an Eye on a Moiety of the Sack, by his political Hint of the other Bottle above, *Line* 22. *More of this* (*i. e.* Sack) *tête a tête.*

O *Phœbus*, *Phœbus*, whether now employ'd
Amidſt the tuneful Nine near *Pindus* Shades
Parnaſſus' Top, or clear *Caſtalian* Stream;
Or haply if the lofty Towers of *Grub-ſtreet*,
Eaſy Deſcent for Gods, delight thee more;
Whence no groſs Fumes of indigeſted Meat
Load the thin Air, or foul the pure ſerene
Thy meagre Vot'ries breath; but grateful Steam
Of vegetable Food, thy Laurel green
Apt Vehicle for Verſe, alike regale
Thy lofty Sons, and their Dominions wide
Extended thro' th' immeaſurable Void.
Here may'ſt Thou deign to dwell, for here the pale
Inhabitant nor hides th' aſpiring Walls

With

With curious Tapestry's inwoven Tale *,
Expensive Ornament, at *Arras* wrought,
Bruges, or *Ghent*, in *Flandria*'s fruitful Fields:
Nor spreads, magnificent, the glitt'ring Hide,
Turgent with Figures emulous of Gold:
But speaking Walls, o'ercast with living Verse,
Resplendent breath the Sentiment elate,
The apt Conceit, and worthy Maze of Wit;
And rising Heroes stalk the nightly Scene,

Man-

* The great *Rhondeletius* differs a little from our Author in his Description of these Mansions; see the following Quotation, by which it plainly appears that some of them were really decorated with *Tapestry.*——I have translated it from the Folio Edition, printed at *Constantinople* by *Typæus:* The critical Reader will find the original Passage in Vol. 37. Pag. 953.

Scriblerus Illustratus.

——————— Exalted high
In Garret vile he lives; with Remnants hung
Of *Tapestry:* But ah! precarious State
Of this vain transient World! all powerful Time!
What dost thou not subdue? see what a Chasm
Gapes wide, tremendous! see where *Saul* enraged,
High on his Throne, encompass'd by his Guards,
With levell'd Spear and Arm extended sits,
Ready to pierce old *Jesse*'s valiant Son,
Spoil'd of his Nose! ————

Mansion of Demi-Gods, 'twixt Earth and Sky,
In Fame recording Charcoal; not the same
Devis'd by mortal Wight, whence Fire exerts
Its fiercest Rage and grinds the pond'rous Ore
To scorching Flames—a glitt'ring Flood of Mischief!
But such as whilom thy own Beams calcin'd,
Thy self howe'er reluctant—when rash *Phaeton*,
Unequal Youth, in evil Hour essay'd
The flaming Car, and whirl'd by rapid Steeds,
Thro' pathless Air, beyond the Mean assign'd,
First thaw'd th' eternal Mounts of rocky Ice
Beneath the frosty Pole; scorch'd *Libia* mourn'd
The needless Fire, and *Latium*'s flow'ry Plain
Became an arid Waste—hard in its Tubes
Dry'd human Life, and thro' the Forest wide
Th' accended Heat devour'd the leafy Race,
Nor spar'd thy *Daphne*; whether near the *Po*
She view'd her Charms; for still the Maid, a Tree,
Explores the glassy Stream, or, near the *Sein*,
Delighted fertile *Gallia*'s sprightly Sons.
But what Excursions breathless do I make
Hunting this Charcoal, tho' immortal Coal
Or Ink my Theme demands—But what's my Theme,
Cynthia or Conquest, *Caucasus* or Court-nights,
Or all, or none—avaunt I soar above ye;

Sublimity ſhall own her aching Sight *
Unable to purſue me; when I dive
Beyond a Comet's Speed, and hiſs with Motion,
I'll teach Profundity herſelf her Shallowneſs.

HOMER and *Pindar* were exalted Bards,
Originals for me! rot Imitators.
I hate them and forbid them—I'm an Extaſy;
Others have dreamt about them—wondrous Tranſports
Mine ſure muſt give my Readers; they're as catching
† At leaſt as Tears—my Service to your *Horace*;

You

* In like manner writeth the learned *Parallellius*, B. 63. which is thus rendered into our Tongue, by the *Illuſtrious Scriblerus*.

————— Rapt in Thought
Fancy preſents before his raviſh'd Eyes
Diſtant Poſterity, upon his Page
With Tranſport dwelling; while bright Learning's Sons
That Ages hence muſt tread this earthly Ball,
Indignant ſeem to curſe the thankleſs Age,
That ſtarv'd ſuch Merit.

N. B. The learned Critic will undoubtedly perceive, that this *Note* is inſerted purely for the ſake of clearing up the Text. *W. W.*

† ——— *Si vis me flere dolendum*
Primum ipſi tibi ——— HOR. ART. POETIC.

You bid me profit too—but dear *Venustan*
What Intercourse has Poetry with Profit?
Mæcenatism's defunct, tho' deathless *Pope*,
With loud Applause has left, and tuneful Care,
What nearly might set up a middling Draper.
No Draper like the Dean, who wrote of Punning,
And *wooden* Coin to purchase *Bulls* in *Ireland*,
Sweet Scene of Turf and Butter—trebly senseless
Ah me! to fancy Writers must have Sense,
When I have read such Writings—nay when *Swift*'s
Brisk Salt, bright Droll, and animated Style
Spire to a Point, then settle in a * *Struldbrug*.
Scribe then ye *Slows*, hum on ye warbling Fry,
Secure from legal Idiocy and *Bedlam*,
While I in Puns pin up your Panegyrick.

Monstrous! such trifling in heroic Strains!
Some Critick grave exclaims, with solemn Mien,
And front full sapient; whose profoundest View
Ill kens our Drift, nor marks our nice Connexion.
To sink and soar's the Contrast, there's the Skill:
Rules may be Nonsense, as we oft have seen
Nonsense full regular; but Flight's a *Genius*.
Whoso's inspir'd must write, ev'n tho' he find

G Little

* See *Gulliver*'s Travels.

Little worth writing on, and writing worth
Still less or nothing. Now, since Tragic Lays
Are really sad; the Comic just ridiculous,
And Pastoral soft and milky, what remains,
But that a Wit or Bard of Taste aspire
To new Device, or deign to write an *Ollio*;
Mental Repast divine! which apt regales
The various Calls of Gust, with sapid Force,
And Irritation keen; while Sense and Nonsense
Alternately approves; while Smiles and Frowns
Consent to disagree; and loud Variety
With wakeful Discord chequers o'er the Scene.

But ah! what knotty Subjects rest unsung
By ev'ry Bard, where Illustration deep
Might crown the richer Page with *Quirks* profound,
And *Quidditi*es of Things, Knowledge occult
Diffusing wide, and cancelling the Poverty
Of simple Intellect with dark Distinction:
Wond'rous the more in this so curious Age,
Devote to Sapience, when the Name of K—gs
On *due Encouragement* is full propense
T' *encourage* Erudition, when Squire *Ayre*,
Aerial Essence, deals in Shillings, Pence,
Memoirs and Patents; while substantial *Curl*
Of Fame so chaste, so justly once erect

In *Norway* Neckcloth, happily transform'd
By ſome of his own *Ovid*'s, reads himſelf,
Regenerate Soul! *Our truſty well beloved.*

But while I mention *Curl*, and deeply ponder
On Modeſty his Attribute—whoſe Form,
Beauteous and lowly, moves, as half receding,
She dreaded Admiration—ſcarce her Vail
Conceals her crimſon Fluſhings—on the Ground
Submiſs ſhe looks, of ſimple Air, and Voice
Low as the ſofteſt Breeze, her Dreſs ſo plain,
She can't appear at Court— In Youth methinks
I've known her—but no more, the fruitleſs Charmer
Still ruins her Poſſeſſors, hence neglected,
How juſtly! nameleſs Bards alone and Authors,
My ſelf and my *Pelagius* ſtill affect her,
Reſigning all the Fame our ſelves might reap
To Porcupines and Quidnuncs; yet perhaps
In this not injudicious, to evade
Critic's dire Morſure,—haply e'en to tempt
Fame's fierce Purſuit by no ill-feign'd Retreat:
While ſeeming coy to Glory we ſecure her
With quaint Addreſs epiſcopal, ambitious
In ſecret to be deem'd to hide our Bluſhes,
While really vain and proud of our Humility.

What crasser Air alas! what grosser *Medium*
Thus damps the Poet's Flight, and nearly makes him
Degen'rate into Sense, and sink to Meaning!
Ye *Moorfield* Sages hail! whom moral *Turks*
Wou'd sagely deem divine, tho' envious Men
Immure, enchain and mortify, for being
More happily delirious than themselves;
Ev'n oft more wise and good—if ye are starv'd,
It is not o'er your Bags—if ye are Monarchs,
Y'e're not insatiate, Crowns of Straw content,
And simplest Cates suffice you—if ye're Patriots,
Ye prove yourselves sincere, in ceaseless Toil
Spending your Faculties for *Britain*'s Weal;
Ye rare, choice Proofs of *British* Incorruption!
If Lovers, ye are delicate and constant,
And the last Gasp sighs out th' obdurate fair one:
Nor useless, tho' immur'd, e'en now perhaps
Your simple Virtues meritorious save
A while our *Sodom*—Virtue's self's thought mad,
Or singular; from honest Sense and Courage
A gen'rous Leader caught a glorious Frenzy.
—It comes, ineffable, sweet, kind Contagion,
Immortal Leaves of Emerald wreath'd with Gold,
Navies of Chrystal, Waves of rosy Nectar
Dance to my Vision—adamantine Breasts,

And

And Eyes, of Glance unſpeakable, confuſe
And bleſs me—Hah! what heav'nly painted Clouds
Array the concave Sky, all looſe and flowing,
The Night Robes of the Sun in *Thetis'* Chambers:
While on the diſtant Mount full ſtately ſhines
The Caſtle all of ruſtleſs poliſh'd Steel,
Maſſy and grand, the Battlements of Gold,
Which with the brazen Gates, the chryſtal Portals,
And Walls of various Agate, neat inlaid,
And fac'd with Iv'ry, gleam another Sun,
And gild the Meads, where num'rous tiny Elves
Scarce preſs the Green; where friſking Satÿrs play
Enamour'd, while three royal Virgins moving
With ſtarry Luſtre, ſmile immortal Graces;
As here they crop the ſilver Primroſe, join'd
To Violets of Amethyſt, commix'd
With many an od'rous lucid Flow'r beſide
Of vegetable Gems, to weave fit Garlands
For three redoubted Knights, now haply journeying,
Thro' many a fierce Adventure, from *Pegu*,
Georgia and *Cachemire*, inform'd by Fame,
Or friendly Sage, of the approaching Liſts,
And the unequall'd Charms of each high Virgin,
Whoſe Smiles muſt crown the Victor's high Atchievment.
What rare Devices ſhine! what Tilts enſue

Within

Within the Barriers! while th' imperial Virgins
Breath ſecret Wiſhes for the bleſt TRIUMVIRADE
So deſtin'd to obtain them; whoſe Demeanour,
High Port, and ſweet Addreſs, at Sight beſpoke
Their Birth, Deſert, and Proweſs, ill conceal'd
Beneath their Armour—Ejulations tear
The azure Vault immenſe—with princely Mien
They kneel to wear their Chaplets—what extatic
Nuptials enſue! I hear th' immortal Strains
Of *Orpheus* and *Muſæus*, for a Time
Exchanging their *Elyſium.* Roſy Wine
I quaff, beyond *Falernium*'s boaſted Juice,
Or *Maſſic* old, modern *Tokay*, *Champaign*,
Cyprus, or *Hermitage*, regale of Monks;
'Till all adown the painted Couch I ſink
In Sleep ideal, when my Bliſs recedes,
The dear Deluſions fly; awak'd and wild,
I find my ſelf, as erſt *Gonzales*, left
By ſome ſagacious *Ganzas* near *Pekin*,
Imperial City—anxious ſtill I doubt
The Scene how real—Worth and Knowledge here
Are ſolely noble—whoſo ſerves the State
Muſt really know, and will, and act her Service—
Obſolete Cuſtoms all, exotic Trifling!

Bleſt

Bleſt be the medic *, Sheep, who firſt, diſcover'd
Arabia's Fruit ſo potable and fragrant,
Which ſocial aggregates, in Mixture bland,
At *George's*, *Richard's*, *Bedford's*, *Tom's* and *Slaughter's*,
The various Brood of Man; while various Themes,
Cricket, Love, Politics, Stocks, Plays, and Battles,
Mix with the tepid Steam; while curious ſome
The Pamphlet of Projector, Peer, or, Starv'ling
Intent peruſe, or cheaply damn; befriended!
With modern Art to further Reading, by
Preventing Writing—Circling round mean while
Inceſſant walks the Library, addreſt
To 'Prentice ſpruce, or aſtrologic Cobler
Nice Millener, or Taylor ſcientific.
Nay haply e'en ſome Toaſt exalted high
In *Bridges-ſtreet*, hence delicately fills
The Vacancies of Love, with Novel ſweet,
Or Verſe luxurious; while the fond Librarian
Viſits her more enamour'd, as her Billets
Are ſcrawl'd in ſofter Terms, and better Spelling;
She liſps more elegant, and ſmiles embelliſh'd.
Pierc'd, like the Eagle, by an Arrow feather'd

From

* Coffee is ſaid to have been firſt diſcover'd, by its exhilarating Effects on ſome Sheep, who brous'd on the Plant in Berry.

From his own Plumage, all inflam'd he rushes
Swift to her Transports; the dissolving fair one
Returns his Flames with many a future Dart
Of pungent Love—thus paying her Subscription.

But all, says *Maro*, are not charm'd with Brambles;
Many the stately various Groves admire,
Whence mighty Fleets, Guns, Swords, dire Stocks, and
Gallows:
Yet chief select the Oak and lofty Pine,
So wont to brace the Ribs, and mast the Hull
Of some bold Cruizer, bent on Trade or Conquest,
To *Afric* or the *Indies*, where the Sand
With granulous Gold's commix'd; or Gales all spicy
Engross the Atmosphere—while yet unfell'd,
Untouch'd their vegetable Woodmates raise
Their Heads green Honours, with extended Arms
Lodging the various Tennants of the Wood.
Whether they hull the sweet nutritious Grain;
Or pry the Bark or Earth for reptile Food;
Or prey on other Volatiles; or pierce
The gelid Brook, or warmer briny Sea,
In quest of fishy Meal, the Perch or Mullet,
Delicious Food! which many an Epicure
May vainly wish, unless consenting Fate

Has

Has with the magic Weight inclin'd his Fob,
Which turns itſelf to all Things, Delicates,
Dreſs, total Worth, Virginities and Boroughs.

Thus have I apt deduc'd a modern Lay;
Nor to my Theme unequal; tho' unaided,
Like many a modern Bard, by gentle *Phœbus*,
And all the tuneful Nine, however mention'd
To decorate my Song—But chief by Thee
Conducted, fair Digreſſion, who, unſparing
Has ſtrew'd with various Flow'rs the ſinuous Way,
And ſafely clu'd thy Bard thro' each *Meander*
Of Fancy's winding Maze—Then may no Critic
Unhallow'd, or tremendous blaſt the Strain
With faſcinating Squint, e'er ſage Reſerve
And Meditation deep aſſure him equal
To our full Scope—Aught if his Judgment meet
It can't approve, let him admire and own
Its bounded Ken; 'twas far from our Intention
With Entertainment to provide him Taſte;
Inſipids feaſt we not—Some Seer prophetic
Of happier Penetration may hereafter
Transfund our myſtic Lines to *Greek* and *Dutch*,
And *Hebrew* and *Chaldaic*, when a certain
Arrangement of the whole, Lines, Words, and Letters,

(*For there the Secret lies*) ſhall ſhew profound
Treaſures of Science, and on ev'ry Subject:
But this the Vice, the Crudity and Darkneſs
Of our vile Age, and the ſaid State of *Europe*
Defers—not leſs ſecure the myſtic Bard
Of lateſt Fame, while, ſmiling Sage, * *Democritus*
Hands me his Fiſt, and ranks me high on *Helicon*.

So when ſome Tempeſt ſweeps the Mountain's Brow,
Or ſporting May-Nymphs celebrate the Feſtal
With Dance and Garland; when the ſcaly Fry
Feed in the lucid Stream; when Ladies weep,
Or laugh, and Aſſes bray, and Poets rhyme;
Or a fierce Hawk devours a puny Bird,
'Tis wondrous clear—NO WONDERS HAVE OCCURR'D.

* ——— *excludit ſanos* Helicone *poetas*
Democritus ——— HOR. ART. POET.

THE

THE

PROCESSIONADE:

In a Panegyri-Satiri-Serio-Comi-Baladical

VERSICLES.

Ecce iterum CRISPINUS! Juv.

By *PORCUPINUS PELAGIUS.*

THE Author being much oblig'd to the Town for the favourable Reception his little Performances have met with, thinks it incumbent upon him, as some late Attempts of the like Kind have been unfairly imputed to him, to declare, that he has publish'd nothing since the TRIUMVIRADE. *He has Reason to complain of having been uncandidly dealt with, in the Publication of a former* Piece, *even yet more successful than the last, with which a Gentleman was pleas'd to make more than a little too free; not only in publishing it without the Author's Privity, but in making such Amputations as greatly interfer'd with the main Design; a great many Lines have been alter'd, and, as the Author conceives, not for the best: And not only that, but even some Characters were entirely omitted, and others unkindly inverted. It shall suffice, for the present, to mention only the first and last Characters in that Piece.*

THE

PROCESSIONADE.

THERE are few unacquainted with th' *old Palace-Hall*,
Tho' happy are those who know't not at all;
Where four ancient Rook'ries, invested with Pow'r,
All the Gold in the Nation and Silver devour.
Sing Tantarara, Rogues all, &c.

Twelve

Twelve Reverend Brethren, diſtinct by their Gowns,
Their Furs, and their Ermin, and Square Copple Crowns,
From among them, ſelected, preſide o'er the reſt,
And, tho' it's oft otherwiſe, ſhou'd be the beſt.

Sing Tantarara, &c.

Superior to theſe is another great Rook,
Call'd Lord *Paramount*, very learn'd in his Book,
Perch'd up on a Spray at the Will of their Kings,
From the reſt well diſtinguiſh'd by Gold on his Wings.

Sing Tantarara, &c.

The Rooks all aſſembl'd, like Sages of Law,
God ſhield every honeſt good Man from its Paw,
To oppoſe a Banditti of plundering Elves,
As the ſole Right of plund'ring they claim to themſelves.

Sing Tantarara, &c.

To the *Eagle*, may Heaven e'er grant him Succeſs,
They clubb'd out a notable loyal Addreſs,
Made a Tender, moſt ſolemn, of Lives and of Purſe,
Tho' they meant no more by't than a *Motion of Courſe*.

Sing Tantarara, &c.

And

And to tell you the Truth, for you know 'tis but civil,
To give e'en his Due to their Patron the D——l;
Th' Addreſs was well penn'd, as to Language and Matter,
Pelagius himſelf could have ſcarce done a better.

Sing Tantarara, &c.

Save, with humble Submiſſion to modern Addreſſes,
He means from his Heart what his Language expreſſes;
Whereas this Parade was no more than to prove,
The mighty Importance their C———r was of.

Sing Tantarara, &c.

From thence to the C——t, they went all in a Row,
In the Spoils of their Country, a terrible Show!
Had all Folks their own, what a Flight had been there
Of mere Fable Crows, all unfeather'd and bare?

Sing Tantarara, &c.

Paramount led the Van, all betufted with Gold,
Which, rejoicing, he oft turn'd his Eyes to behold,
The Steed in the Team more delighted ne'er ſwells,
While he leads in the Traces bejingl'd with Bells.

Sing Tantarara, &c.

If no P—l—ti—n, to fence 'gainſt the *French*,
Yet as able a Chief as e'er perch'd on the Bench;
His Hands, ſome aſſert, are as clean as his Face,
The reſt you will hear when he's out of his Place.

Sing Tantarara, &c.

The *Eagle* the loyal Addreſs well receiv'd,
But aſtoniſh'd to ſee what could ſcarce be believ'd;
Much pity'd his Subjects, ſo num'rous a Band
Of Birds, with ſuch Talons, ſhould prey o'er the Land.

Sing Tantarara, &c.

The Twelve into Fours, drew up equal and certain,
The Chief like a Dove, and the next like a *Martin*;
A free *Denizen* That, all preferr'd for their Worth,
And a bold *Anti-Codex*, long dormant, the Fourth.

Sing Tantarara, &c.

Quo' the *Eagle*, who's that with his honeſt old Face,
His Wings, like your Lordſhip's, beſpangl'd with Lace?
And who ſhould it be but the Law in its Wane,
Expreſs'd in his Honour of *C——ry-L—e*.

Sing Tantarara, &c.

How-

However, a Rook of Politeneſs and Taſte,
His Officers too, as to Gains very chaſte,
Obligingly careful, no proud ſilly Novice,
Like a *Paramour* Coxcomb in Common-Law Office.

Sing Tantarara, &c.

And here, reſum'd he, is the Law in his Strength,
Expreſs'd in the other Chief J—ſt—'s Length;
I find he treads cloſe on your Heels for the M——,
And waits, like a Cat o'er a Chink, for your Place.

Sing Tantarara, &c.

For This and for That, and for moſt Things he's fit,
For the Bench he has Law, for the Court he has Wit,
For the Camp can aſſume a bold Coll'nel-like Air,
And has wond'rous good *natural Parts* for the Fair.

Sing Tantarara, &c.

Then preſenting his worthy Aſſociates all Three,
An *Has-been* This here, That a *Never-will-be*;
But from *Grumbler* and *Conſul*, and *State-Pampbleteer*,
The Third is turn'd out in his Law pretty clear.

Sing Tantarara, &c.

I *Tom*

Tom Rook with his Phiz ſomewhat learnedly ſour,
Was aſham'd, with his Three Harlequins, to make Four.
Their Coats were bechequer'd, juſt like their Decrees,
Right and wrong is the ſame as to Wages and Fees.

Sing Tantarara, &c.

'Tis whiſper'd, however, this Reverend Dozen,
For the Good of the Realm ſo judiciouſly choſen,
So gravely array'd in their Copples and Geers,
Complain'd of their Salaries long in Arrears.

Sing Tantarara, &c.

Next theſe introduc'd, was the *Prime* 'mong the Coif,
Who *blaz'd in the Face* like ſome Saracen Wife,
Fam'd firſt for betraying in Public his Truſt,
And then over-reaching Sir *Bob* for a Poſt.

Sing Tantarara, &c.

His Brethren all rang'd in a Line on each Side,
Out of Countenance much for their Premier Guide,
Be-perr'wig'd all o'er in heroic Array,
Like ſo many *Quins* or *Delanes* in a Play.

Sing Tantarara, &c.

Tho'

Tho' 'twas formerly ſaid, that the Coif was the Stage,
Like an Hoſpital modern, for caſt-off old Age;
Yet that now the whole Order are Conj'rers we ſee,
And can tell us the Event of a Cauſe by a Fee.

Sing Tantarara, &c.

Then Lord *Paramount*, ſingling little Sir *Dud*,
Said, tho' for his Poſt he was proper and good,
Yet if he roſe higher he'd ſink in the Scene,
And his Figure and Aſpect are rather too mean:

Sing Tantarara, &c.

And here is Sir Knight, who ſtands firſt at the Bar,
Look round o'er the Rook'ries you'll find not his Par,
Deſpiſing Preferment, he quitted his Poſt,
To ſhew by his Succeſſor what we have loſt.

Sing Tantarara, &c.

This new-fangl'd *Scot*, who was brought up at Home,
In the very ſame School as his Brother at *Rome*,
Kneel'd, conſcious, as tho' his old Comrades might urge,
He had formerly drank to the *King* before *George*.

Sing Tantarara, &c.

Ill betide those that prais'd, premature, in the South,
As a Genius this Mushroom of North-Country Growth:
Who from flashing a little at first pretty smart,
Now expires with a Sound and a Stink like a F——t.

Sing Tantarara, &c.

And this is my *African* Fav'rite *Tom Cl—ke*,
Tho' dirty complexion'd, yet keen as a Shark,
His affected Grimace, and his Gesture and Shrug,
Denote him a Kind of a Male *Molly Mogg*.

Sing Tantarara, &c.

That's little *Brunetto*, so dapper and stiff,
A faithful Relator of all in his Brief;
If unheated by Fees he too languidly pleads;
And tho' often speaks well, yet too facil recedes.

Sing Tantarara, &c.

The Middle-Bar Gentry pass'd Muster along,
But the *Eagle* perceiving, the *Fritlings* among,
A rusty, audacious, broad, bell-mettle Front,
Enquir'd who it was of my Lord *Paramount*.

Sing Tantarara, &c.

Why

Why hur is a *King*, who, Cot-ſplut all her Nails,
Was a Kind of a Mountebank Doctor in *Wales*,
But tir'd of inſpecting old Women's Cloſe-ſtools,
Hur now 'mong the Rook'ries at *Weſtminſter* prowls.

Sing Tantarara, &c.

Then higgledy-piggledy forward they preſt,
T' evince how they all did Rebellion deteſt:
With his Sword, in an Inſtant, his Majeſty ſmites,
No leſs, o'er the Shoulders, than Six Simple Knights.

Sing Tantarara, &c.

Neglected poor Honour! derided by Wits,
Now courted alone by the Rooks and the Cits,
And eke by ſome *Weſtminſter* Juſtice of Peace,
As witneſs the Three on the former Addreſs.

Sing Tantarara, &c.

Well pleas'd all our Rooks in Proceſſion return'd
Eſpecially thoſe with new Honours adorn'd;
Next *Sunday* they went in a Row to the Church,
And among all my Ladies, my good *Lady B—ch*.

Sing Tantarara, &c.

Who's

Whe's mortify'd much in the Midſt of her Joys,
To find that her Title, 'mong Girls and Boys,
Is terribly fear'd, that her Ladyſhip ſcarce
Can appear, but they cry, *Aware Hawk*, for the A—ſe.

Sing Tantarara, &c.

THE

THE

'PISCOPADE:

A Panegyri-Satiri-Serio-Comical

POEM.

By *PORCUPINUS PELAGIUS.*

Qui capit ille facit. OVID.

PREFACE.

THE *following is a Translation from the* Spanish *of Don* Francisco Pedro de Lopez, *an* Asturian *by Birth. It is said to have been written during the last Vacancy of the Capital See of* TOLEDO; *which was since conferred on Don* Lewis, *third Son of the late King of* Spain, *by the present Queen Dowager; as much distinguished for his* pious *good Qualities, as his Mother for those of Meekness and Condescension.*

As to the Verse; in Quantity, it consists of eleven Syllables, and sometimes of twelve, according to the Run of the Line when it makes no Difference on the

K *Ear.*

Ear. In Quality, it is Burlesque, and generally used in humorous Compositions; which, like all other Burlesques, requires to be humoured in the Reading; as it is hardly practicable to arrange Words in it properly accented, according to their Sense and Construction: For if a Line does not hit well in its first natural Flow, an Amendment for the Sake of Accent, serves only to make it hobble. I have known three different Persons read the same Line in three different Ways, and each Reading seemed agreeable to the Ear. The candid Reader, who has a Mind to be diverted, will therefore suffer this Observation to direct his reading humorous Verse after an humorous Way, as there is no other Rule to go by.

The Translator has, after the Manner of Philips's Don Quixot, *frequently substituted* English *Names and Terms instead of* Spanish *ones; the better to accommodate the vulgar Reader, and give him a more familiar Idea of the Author's Humour: Therefore, as often as they occur, they must be considered accordingly, and not as of any thing that happened in* England.

THE

'PISCOPADE.

THE Cabinet, ſummon'd, in Council
conven'd,
Prodigious Conſtituents! anſw'ring the
End;
Profound Politicians, ſagaciouſly ſage!
Who govern by Noſtrums the politic Stage:
Like *Turner* and *Rock* in the phyſical Train,
Each conſiders himſelf the great Stateſman of *Spain*,
Who can ſhape out the Public alone on the Anvil,
This here is a *Burleigh*, that there is a *G * **.

As ſupreme of the Board, high aloft in the Air,
Don Præſes del Dorſo gave Law from the *Chair*;

Where

Where late he had voted his Son out of Poſt,
To keep himſelf in with the Lords of the Coaſt:
Soporiferous there, very lordly he ſate,
Like a Judge on the Bench, when a Trial hangs late.

Then *Gow'ron Transfugos*, conforming ſo humbly,
Who had firſt diſplac'd *H**y*, and afterwards *C**y*;
Moſt ſtrangely bedumpt, took his Place at his Heels,
And, as *Lockit* his Irons, bejingled his *Seals*:
Diſcontent and Reflection imbitter'd his Face,
As tho' he ſeem'd griev'd he went down to the Race.

On his Left, ſate *Don Juan*, protub'rately big!
For he follows his Sire like a *Tantony* Pig;
Chriſt-Croſſes, at leaſt to th' Amount of a Score;
Marks doloreus, ah! on his Shoulders he bore;
In ſevere Conſtigation, ſome ſay, they were done,
For the Honour of *Turncoats* laid furiouſly on.

Next him, ſat the Coaſter *Don Tom del Vagary*,
Cheek-by-Joul with his Brother, Great *Gentleman Harry*;
Like *Caſtor* and *Pollux*, alternately ſhining,
Or rather, unlike them, together declining.

Don Caſtro del Pratum, a Wit heretofore!
But, ſince he has *coaliz'd*, Wit is no more;

In

In the Right of his Station among them attends,
Much asham'd of himself, his *old* Foes, and *new* Friends;
All his old Brother Authors look'd on him oblique,
Pair'd his Coat with *Don Juan*'s, and thought them alike:
His lost Appellation of Patriot they mourn'd,
'Till *Pelagius* assur'd them *his Coat was not turn'd.*
And that soon they would find him withdraw from his Place,
Redistinguished with Honour and courtly Disgrace;
Give some future *Cadwallader* Colour to tell,
He writes his new Paper—and so make it sell. *

In the Rear of th' Assembly sat *Bronzo* o'ercast,
His *Honour*'s most tractable Piece of Puff-paste!
Very ready to take what Impression he'd give,
So the *S—f—d* Petition he might but survive:
Inscrib'd, thro' an Hypocrite Veil, on his Face,
Might be read, *A Devise in Remainder—and Place:*
Edentula's Jordan he held in his Hand,
The Tenure annex'd to his new-stolen Land;
Most sav'ry and od'rous however it smell'd!
Like the Tax which *Vespasian* on Urine compell'd.

Their

* 'Tis observable the *Grubeans* of *Madrid* used to make free with this noble *Don*'s Name, to give Currency to their political Productions.

Their Businefs was not to confer 'gainst the Foe,
Nor yet some immoderate Tax to forgoe;
Nor how to consult, in his virtuous Recefs,
Olivarez Count Hawnes, to sketch out a Peace;
Not so; — for th' Occasion was merely domestic,
And, what may be wonder'd at, — Ecclesiastic!
But, on serious Reflection, the Wonder grows lefs,
For it was on the learned *Arch-Pontiff*'s Decease;
Great Sire of *Toledo!* — departed that Morn,
To pay the just Debt, which to pay he was born:
To consider with whom they should fill up his Place,
And dubb with the Stile of *Pontifical Grace.*

The *Chair* declar'd loudly *Londono* the Man,
Let us gain him, quo' he, for a Friend if we can.

Obj.] The learned *Londono* more honour'd than lov'd,
With some little Restriction might well be approv'd,
Had he not, in his Volume, exhibited forth
Proud Lady *Ecclesia*'s high Power and Worth;
Hight *Codex*, huge Treatise! and then made a Handle
Of Conscience to keep out poor Infidel *R*——.

Anf.]

Anf.] 'Twas right! he receiv'd Information, not
fought;
Confiftent his Deed with the Doctrine he taught;
Remifs is that Shepherd who'd lazily fleep,
And let in the Wolf 'mongft his innocent Sheep.
Inflexibly juft! who believ'd not the Word
He repell'd with his mighty *Whip-Sillabub* Lord!
Of extenfive fine Parts oftentatioufly vain,
Yet perplex'd in maturing, and apt to o'erftrain;
'Tho' prompt of Conception, yet hard to believe
Whofe Skill might miflead, and Experience deceive;
Both Favour and Juftice to fuch he deny'd,
And never forgave who eluded his Pride.
His Reas'ning had pleas'd if not carried too far,
And that he affected t' o'ermatch all the B *.
Tho' a Genius and quick in the Art of difcerning,
Yet fhort of his plain Predeceffor in Learning:
'Tis as bad, when the Race at *Newmarket* is loft,
In the Horfe that o'erfhoots, as falls fhort, of the Poft.
Tho' great 'mong the *Knowing* he ne'er was allow'd,
Yet he whipp'd up a Sillabub well for the Crowd.

While thus in Debate, as he'd Right to be there,
His *Grandeur* came in, and gave Thanks to the *Chair*.

No

No *Breaſt-plate* he wore, like the firſt of the Trade,
With the Myſt'ry and A*t of R*l*g*n inlaid;
But an high tow'ring M**re, with *Mahomet*'s Arms!
Not Ch*t's, as expreſs'd in ſymbolical Terms;
Gules, Rapiers a Brace in Saltire, Argent, he bore,
But the Pommels were Chriſtian, becauſe they were *Or!*
He declar'd, that, with Age and Infirmities worn,
He, inſtead of Promotion, expected an Urn;
That as, once in Diſcharge of his Conſcience and Truſt,
He miſs'd of the Station by giving Diſguſt,
He now had the Pleaſure in Turn to refuſe,
Reſpectfully begging, howe'er, their Excuſe:
That an old Piece of Parchment he found on his File,
Expreſs'd, beyond Doubt, it was hardly worth while.

Tho' the Board was ſurpriz'd the Refuſal to hear,
Yet with Reaſon allowing the *Nolo* ſincere,
Caſt their Thoughts upon *Tomo Superbos* the next,
For in Right of a Hint he'd a kind of Pretext.
This Lawyer's great Maſter, high Churchman elate!
Erſt Antagoniſt bold in *Bangorian* Debate,
Very learn'd! very big! very haughty and proud!
Might undoubtedly do very well, if he wou'd;
Be of Uſe to the C * h, — and the Court at a Pinch,
Perplex the Debate, and an Argument clinch:

As once he oppos'd, in ſignificant Words,
Th' Independence of Parliament, C**ns and L*ds!

As the Council was going to make out his Fiat,
Came in *Cabellano*,—My Lords, pray be quiet,
Well I know that his *Grandeur*, on hearing th' Alarum,
Has caſt up the Odds 'twixt *Toledo* and *S ***,
Taking in all his other Preferments ſo ample,
Lord *A*m*n*r*, Ch*c'l*r, Maſter o' th' *T* **;
How much he's to pay, and how long he muſt live
To regain his Diſburſements, e'er Death may arrive;
As 'twill hardly quit Coſt, he would fain be excus'd;
Beſides, he'll not take what *Londono* refus'd.

More ſtunn'd and aſtoniſh'd the Council appear'd,
Ambition ſubſiding and Av'rice preferr'd!
That the Lovers of Pow'r, and of Right to command,
Should the Station of Greatneſs one Moment withſtand!
Tho' the firſt might decline it from Profit expectant,
Yet why ſhould the latter appear ſo reluctant?
'Tis ſaid 'twas to bargain for *one* to ſucceed him;
But the Council catch'd hold of his *Nolo*, and chid him,
Proceeded to think and conſider of others,
Who'd more tractably cringe with the Views of the *Brothers*;

So deliver'd a Lift of the Prelates to *S* * ,
To read out diftinctly their Names one by one.

S. *Imprimis*, my Brother, his Grace of *A***,
Vers'd, able, and learn'd, in the *Tennis-court* Law;—
Pfhaw, (anfwer'd the *Chair*, in a Fret and a Pother)
He's a Pontiff already — Damn you and your Brother!
The *Chair* will not fuffer you here t' impofe,
Or be led like your Patron about by the Nofe:
To him you may dictate Preferments and Pofts,
But here you're not Lord-Paramount of the Coafts:
That your Brother had Merit all well might difcern,
And deferv'd Tranfportation—but not to *Hibern*.
Read only their *Grandeurs* of *Spain* my good Friend,
And begin, as in Politics we, at the End.

S. *Pedro Burgos* ftands junior, cognomine *T***
Who is come in at laft, with our laft latter *Lammas*.

Obj.] Avant! quo' *Vagary*,—he's brought in by the K*
And we muft not indulge him too oft in a Thing;
If we grant him an Inch, he'll not reft at an Ell,
Who then will be topmoft we know very well!
But the Man has enough, for he holds *in Commendam*,
Refidentiary, Canonry, Rectory *quondam*.

S. *Of*-

S. *Osbaldo Carleolum*, full far in the *North*:
Obj.] Already his Fortune's of very great Worth!
All the Blessing, like *Jacob*, he stole from his Sire,
And left his poor Brother to wade in the Mire;
Yet Heaven, like *Esau*, enrich'd the Depriv'd,
Who, by good Application and Industry, thriv'd.
Or whether he piously meant to defraud,
Like the Pat*ch, his Brother, his Sire, and his God;
Or whether the Deed was his Father's Caprice,
'Till he shares with his Brother he never shall rise.

Sacerdos Bassishaw, new Pontiff *del Exon*:
Obj.] When th' Obscure are preferr'd 'tis enough for to
vex-one;
Some proud *Predicator* of very small Fame,
For 'till late at St. *Paul*'s we've ne'er heard his Name;
A Citizen-Friar, retailing in Trade
The A*t and the Myst'ry of holy Parade:
He jobb'd with the *Brothers*, got in at a Leap
To a *Crook*, made but rarely Preferment's first Step;
Tho' *Voisie*, with high and iniquitous Hand,
Sacrilegiously sold away most of the Land.
There rest he content, an odd Instance of Luck!
As his *Grandeur* was rais'd out of Citizen Muck.

S. *Don Vor-Tre Meneven*, on th' Edge of the Coast
Where the *Bishop and Clerks* their Antiquity boast;
Obj.] Where from *Aff* fled the Pontiff t' avoid *Saxon* Forage,
And potent brown Ale gives th' Inhabitants Courage;
Where the present Lord *Flamen*, by Brotherly Pow'r,
Over Learning and Merit broke open the Door.
If the Sire was disbench'd, as they tell us the Story,
And excluded from *Grace* as an high-flying *Tory*,
How comes it his Children 'mong *Whigs* should meet Favour?
Why the Cock veer'd about — 'twas a notable Shaver!
Further notic'd this Son may perhaps be in Time,
So sparkish, so beauish, so pert, and so trim!

S. *Don Clericos Bonos*, on *Aricon*'s Flood ——
Obj.] To be sure a good Scholar — by Name — and by Blood!
A Divine by Descent, from St. *Alban* deriving,
A Quality *Flamen*, no doubt on't believing:
Notwithstanding all these, yet he is not the Saint,
Who we mean for the Service of State to transplant.
He will find no Translation in the Year *Forty-seven*,
And perhaps in no other—than that into Heaven.

Take

Take Heed all ye Scholars of *Ox* and of *Cam*,
If the Quality thus will put in for the Game,
Bid adieu to your Books, Studies, Terms and Degrees,
Your Fellowships, Headships, and proud monkish Ease,
Introductive of Mitres; for soon will be seen,
That Title without, and not Merit within,
High Blood, and not Learning, good Sense and Discernment,
Will prove the right Road in the C*h to Preferment:
Perhaps the small M*tres of *Ha*y* the Eight',
May th' Acceptance of Learning and Piety wait;
But believe me the first and the second Rate Flocks,
Will fall to the Share of High-Blood—and the Pox.

S. *Samelo Prænomenos*, Lord Flamen *d'Elwensis*—
Obj.] There *Isaac* puff'd up ministerial Offences,
There *Parsew* embezzled, and *Geoffry*, forsooth!
Is said t'ave been free with historical Truth.
Our Apostle of *Smyrna* abroad went to preach,
And to trade out a little in what he could teach;
Made *Archi-decanos* by *Pontifex W**
Bid since into *Cambria* himself to betake;
And there he must deprecate long for the Sins
Of *Parsew* and *Isaac*, in *Piety* Twins!

S. *Toma-*

S. *Toma-ſino de Lindos*, where erſt we are told,
The Devil o'erlook'd both the Town and the Fold.—

Obj.] The Objection is ſtrong, 'tis preſum'd, againſt him,
In hunting Preferment he fractur'd a Limb;
In haſtening along to his Patron, before
His approaching Competitor came to the Door,
He trod on his Caſſock, and fell in the Street,
And down went Canonicals into the Pit.
By Experience grown wiſer and eaſy to boot,
He will hardly be tempted to riſk t'other Foot,
To remove from a Place where he's lov'd and extoll'd;
Clean ſweeps the new Broom —— Heav'n ſend he may hold!

S. *Hut-Ton de Ban-Gorio*, in th' Hills of *Aſture*,
Where of Courſe all the Natives are Gentlemen pure
By Patent from Heaven,——
Obj.] That City, or near it,
Was fam'd for oppoſing proud *Auſtin* with Spirit,
Where, refuſing t' acknowledge the *Pope*, the good Saint
Sent the Monks up to Heaven to make their Complaint.
Fam'd too for *Pelagius*, as Hiſtory tells,
And the old Flamen *Bulkley* who ſold off the Bells.

But

But as grandeural *Mat* is allow'd of good Note,
His Relatives num'rous respectively vote,
Tho' he fails of *Toledo*, we'll find him a Place,
Perhaps by and by, with the Title of *Grace!*
To the *Ouse** from the *Menai*† is no unknown Run,
Th' Example is recent, for lately 'twas done.

S. *Necroman del Hocus Fontanensis et Bathon*——
Obj.] Nor in *Askelon* publish, nor tell it in *Gathon*,
That, among all our *Reverendini* around,
There's, bless us! but one single Conjurer found!
Great Things he can do!——Ropes of Sand he can spin,
'Twas he that decypher'd the Dog *Harlequin*;
Expounded the Letters, unravell'd the Jest,
Made a Plot of a Woman, a Dog, and a Priest;
Bound all the long Alphabet fast in a Link,
And by Subsequents prov'd what Precedents might think;
Saw reverend Treason in Prayers prelatic,
And good Mrs. *H** yes* at the Bottom aquatic;
Saw all that *Leviathan* wish'd might be seen,
The *Pastor* depriv'd — and himself made a D*;

Next

* In *Spanish*, the *Ebro*.
† The Straits of *Gibraltar*.

Next preferr'd to a *Crook* — then translated to *W**
Where he's like to remain 'till *Don John* has the *Seals.*

S. *Gil Borto Piscopulos Blunderan dell Aff:* ——
Obj.] A sufficient tho' moderate *Grandural Staff*;
(Thank th' extravagant *Dunstan*, the same, I suppose,
Who took with the Tongs the poor De'il by the Nose)
Without the long Train of Preferments which *K**, †
In his *elegant Latin* ‡ annex'd to the *Thing*:
Grave et plumbum — said the *Jacobite* Laic—
Such a Weight of Preferments o'erpowers the weak:
'Tis the Fate of the C*h to be ever abus'd,
Dunciadi distinguish'd, and Merit refus'd!
While These strut in *Purple* and wallow in Riches,
Those hide, in poor *Cassocks*, the Absence of Breeches.
Still his *Weight* will exalt him! nay is't not agreed
He's to pass from the *Taaf* 'twixt the *Tees* and the *Tw*d?* ‖

S. *Chi-*

† Archidiaconus, Præbendarius, Custos, Augur, Rector, Prolocutor, Flamen Major, Flamen Minor, Flamen Dialis, Flamen Cæsaris, Rusticus, Urbanus, Aulicus, Academicus, &c.

‡ Epistola Objurgatoria.

‖ In *Spanish* the *Guadelquivir*, the *Douro*, and *Garron.*

S. *Chi-Castrum Ben. Coll. Cantab. Matathias*——
Obj.] He had always to govern a natural Bias:
He travell'd from *Cam* to old *Taase*, and from thence
To *Cissa*'s proud City, erst strong for Defence!
His Outside exhibits a good likely Sign,
A Mark that he's not over-furnish'd within;
Howe'er, if no Conj'rer, he's not a bad Man,
He gives us his Vote, and submits to our Plan,
He is quiet and easy, and bounds his Desire,
And seems not to court a Translation that's high'r.

S. *Usephos Cellarion*, his *Grandeur* of *B* * *,
Where Pebbles are found quite as clear as a Christal:—
Obj.] He is busy disbursing of Money good Store,
In repairing, where never Repairs were before;
Their dilapidate *Grandeurs*, preceding, appear
To have minded the Profits much more than Repair;
To pay Master *Paul* by the robbing poor *Peter*,
I've frequently heard of,—*it serves for my Metre*;—
But ne'er of converting the Dues of St. *Paul*,
To eke out a *See* insufficiently small.
Tho' an early Conformist, yet still he *dissents*,
Not pockets, but shares with the C * h in her Rents.

'Till his Buildings are finiſh'd, there let him remain,
In Support of *Lord Flamen* he'll break Mr. *D* *.

S. *Norvicos del Tomo Orien-Anglos de G* *: ——
Obj.] He no ſooner ſet up, than he ſet down, his Coach;
When, diſmounted in Ruins, *Bentleon* did view it,
He inſcrib'd it, inſultingly, *Hic currus fuit!*
He ſtill, *ſemper idem*, in College had tarried,
Had he not to *Severia*'s fair Siſter been married;
Pinn'd cloſe to his Brother-in-Law's brawny Back,
He wound him aloft, as our Cooks do a Jack.
He expects not at preſent a further Advance,
Save by Riſe of that Brother, or ſome other Chance;
Unleſs he can hit it with *Ch*dl*r*, and get
The Diſſenters, like Partridge, to lie for the Net.

S. *Bos-Furius Preſbyteron:* ——
Obj.] - He knew how to trim,
And has got to his laſt, and no higher ſhall climb;
His *firſt* he attain'd to by goſſipping Stories,
By *Corruption and Brib'ry*, his *laſt*, 'gainſt the *Tories*;
Was advanc'd in the *Order* for that very Thing,
For which he ſhould rather have met with a String.
Let him gratefully clear with the *Scots* and their College,
Whence he ſtole his Divinity, Learning and Knowledge;
Where,

Where, forſaking his Cheeſecakes, his Tarts and his
Cuſtards;
Delight of Lord-Mayors and old City-Buſtards!
He took up the painful Profeſſion of Letters,
And learn'd it was meet to *conform* like his Betters.

S. Then comes on his *Grandeur*, learn'd *Ker-ſec del Oxon*,———
Obj.] Once ſuſpected of putting the Garb of a Fox-on;
Who withdrew, from whence Dignity was not in Call,
And wiſely conform'd where a M**re might fall.
But ſhould this be the Man, who ſo frequently preaches,
And ſeems to believe in the Doctrine he teaches,
He may raiſe in the Church ſuch a primitive Cuſtom,
As will little agree with the Sons of *Chryſoſtom*.

S. Meek *Marton Ben-Sonos* ſtands next on the Liſt:—
Obj.] Tho' as good a Lord *Paſtor* as e'er did exiſt,
And deſerves to be rais'd to a M**re that's fatter;
But he's not the Man that muſt go o'er the Water;
Tho' right for our Purpoſe, by Abſence of Spirit,
Yet very unfit from his ſanctified Merit.
Should he chance to oppoſe us, the Crowd, I'll aſſure ye,
Will be full of my very good Lord *C****y*,
Will daily about him for Bleſſing reſort,
For the Bleſſing's enhanc'd that oppoſes the C * t;

Impolitic therefore to make him our Master,
Let him walk then with God in his City of *G**r*.

S. *Avaro del Bottson Paramontos d' l'Isle* :——
Obj.] As he travell'd from *Nor* to the South of the Stile,
Half the Fine, which he'd rais'd to exorbitant Rate,
Departing, he graciously offer'd t' abate,
So he might but enseal and deliver his Deed,
E'er th' Arrival of him who was nam'd to succeed.
My Kingdom is all of this World is his Text,
So that This he enjoys, he ne'er cares for the Next.

S. Tough *Pep-Los Devana Nor-Occidentalis* :——
Obj.] Pursu'd and pursuing with reverend Malice;
T' ep*sc*p*te never he'd met with a Call,
Had he not been assaulted by mad Parson *Paul*;
Had *Gastron* been easy—so fam'd for his Knowledge!—
He'd still been but Warden of *M***r* College;
Had the Rebels Success, and our Gen'rals been hang'd,
'Tis *Paul* had been *Flamen*, and *Pep-Los* had hang'd.

S. *Tyrannos del Rivulet* :——
Obj.] Long since wish'd in Heaven,
Or that never he'd quitted his Sire's native Oven;
Illiberal *Flamen!* the more is the Pity,
Both of this and of that Patriarchate old City;

One

One fam'd for the Taylor, in Statue still living,
For wantonly peeping at Madam *Godiving*,
Who could ne'er, like another *Actæon*, meet Pardon,
For eying the Fruit in the Midst of the Garden;
Sad Monuments both, to the Mortal who'd dare
Be curiously busy with Woman's Affair!
T'other ever renown'd for good Races in Fame,
And giving a late hearty *Drubbing-Bout* Name:
So cautious the Priest that he weighs e'en his *God*,
Which he never receives 'till the Odds are allow'd;
King *Nebuchad's* Image! but yet when he prays,
He ne'er minds the Ballance, nor makes his Essays:
His Pen, so laborious and learnedly dull!
The *Infidel's* Labour establish'd in full,
Instead of o'erthrowing;—Cast his Book at his Head,
For an Ounce of good Silver he's a Pound of dull Lead,
Mere Dough, like the Baker of *Hereford's* Bread.

S. *Dulmanos Wilcocion* stiff Flamen *deR offens*:——
Obj.] He has long in the Abbey interr'd many Coffins!
In Person officiating ever to win-ye,
In Defraud of the Prebend, the Ring and the Guinea;
A Noun Substantive *Crook*, which alone cannot stand
Without a Noun Adjective *D*nry* at Hand:

The

The Abbey of *Thorney* and Mitre of *Roch**,
Can, ſupporting each other, maintain a good Coach.
A Man-of-War *Praymaſter* erſt, where tho' oft
They call on the Devil, yet keep him *abaſt*.
From the *Severn* he travell'd to *Medway* and *Thames*,†
And there he is like to continue it ſeems;
Propitiouſly Chance has made more than his Wiſh-up,
For ſure he could hardly e'er hope to be B**.

S. *Candelarion Avaros*,—who wrote many Reams!
His vain Predeceſſor and he in Extremes;
This wond'rouſly ſparing, and That moſt profuſe;
Odd Oppoſites both, and without juſt Excuſe:
This hoards up his Treaſure from Light and the Day,
That contracted new Debts which he ne'er meant to pay—
The Aſſertion is falſe! they were paid by the Son;—
A little, indeed, by Lord *Froth* was begun,
T' acquire a good Name, forſooth!—nothing more.
When *Edros* prevails by the Pray'rs of the Poor,
And behaves, in the Eye of the World, ſomewhat ſager,
We may then give Attention to him and his *Wager*.

S. We have varied from Order and Rank in the Text,
Take however *Ben los Liberalis* the next;——

Obj.]

† The *Minho*, the *Guadiana*, and the *Tagus*.

Obj.] Erst Maker of Sermons and Joutnal Discourse,
Than These nothing better, than Those nothing worse;
Defender of Treaties, *H*n*v*r's* and *Seville's*,
Leviathan's Schemes, indefensible Evils!
Deceiv'd into these, he will never forget,
Nor be catch'd any more in the Minister's Net.
He is happy and easy, and thinks himself so,
A Scholar, Divine, and a Gentleman too!
He will feast with the Rich, and he'll feed with the Poor,
And welcome attends all who come to his Door;
His Demeanor is affable, kind and endearing,
And he lives like *Trelawney* in all Things—but swearing:
But yet should he controvert aught in the State,
He will stiffly dispute, for he loves a Debate!
Not unlike, in one Way, to the Fair when they scold,
For he'll have the last Word, and will ne'er be controll'd.

Then *Bronso* rose up,—mighty Rival of *Quin!*—
As wak'd from Reflection whom next to take in,
What Master, what Party, what Friend to betray:—
O Sages! quo' he, hear what *Bronso* can say
For bashful Desert, long oppos'd by the Malice
Of the Magistrate's Hand, and the Sons of the Chalice;
Whose Tossings, Repulses, Impris'nings and Woe,
Serve only t' imbrighten and not to o'erthrow;
Laborious,

Laborious, good Man! both in Preaching and Pray'r,
Well read, if not learn'd; great *Flamen* of *Clare!*
Who th' untractable Butcher succesſfully ſtuns,
Inſtructs in Conundrums and Libels in Puns;
Who, like *Paul* in the Midſt of th' *Athenians*, can preach,
And perhaps as ſincere—and as bold in his Speech!
To whom I'm indebted for all my Acqueſts,
In the Art of Perſuaſion—my Actions, my Reſts,
My Flights and my Sinkings, Obſervance of Time,
All theſe I'm indebted, O Sages! to him.
To my humble Requeſt I entreat you concede,
Let my good Brother Orator *Leyhen* ſucceed.
How well will the M*tre his Forehead enſconſe,
Deck his large awful Brows and his reverend *Bronſe!*
'Twill effectually put to his Project a Stop,
Spoil his Talent for preaching and ſhut up his Shop:
For, give but a Prieſt high Preferment, be ſure
He ſeldom is heard above once in his Cure.

His Grace *del Vagary* oppos'd with his Babble,
And declar'd he had libell'd his Cook and his Table,
His Oleo's, Diſguiſings, Ragoûts *alamode*,
And his Belly beſide, moſt adorable God!
And that to the State, 'twas of no ſmall Concernment,
T' exclude Men of Wit from all Hopes of Preferment;

The

The *Reſtorer of th' old Elocution*, perhaps,
Might reſtore true Religion, and ſhew where we
lapſe.

Since from the *Right Grandeutral* Rank you have fell,
Says another, e'en drop the whole *Order* as well;
I'll name you a Laic, as in Caſes ſo urgent
A Judge for the Purpoſe is firſt made a Serjeant,
Who from th' Impoſition of Hands may receive
His Commiſſion at once, to preach and believe.
As already he ſeems to have ſwill'd up a Drench
Of Scripture, ſufficient to poſe all the *Bench*.
Need I mention his Name who has made ſuch a Buſtle,
With his Pen and his Ink for the Gentile Apoſtle;
Who would ſilence the Preſs againſt all but his Muſe,
Which has lately emerg'd on a puerile Cruize,
Call'd at ev'ry old claſſical River's Abode,
In ſorrowful Murmurs, t' attend his *Monode*.

A Hubbub enſued, ſome cried out a Jeſt!
And ſome declar'd loudly for *Gilbo de Weſt*;
While others, more leadenly weighty, thought fit
To hollow for good Mother *Oſburne de Pit*,
Who had ſtill in the Station of Flogger remain'd,
Had he happily never the Scripture profan'd;

To the dull *Norfolk Faction*, in Custody led,
He, instead of Correction, rencontred good Bread:
So he ne'er on the Heels of the Minister trod,
He might, with Impunity, libel his G * d.
Like Brother-Trade *Priscus*, alias *Jeffrey Broadbottom*,
Whom his *Grace* and his *Honour* have pension'd, G*d rot'em,
For abusing his S*v*r*n in *Billingsgate* Rout,
(As *Bronso* within, so did *Priscus* without.)
Thus both met Preferment, instead of a String,
This for libelling G*d, That defaming his King!

The *Chair* interpos'd in a solemn Address,
Full of Wisdom and Learning, as well you may guess!
Reduc'd into Order the vagrant Discourse,
And confin'd it, like Marriage, for better for worse,
To the Rank of Lords *Flamen*, from whence must succeed
Some tractable Father to fill up *Tolede*.

Arch-Halec Eborac long Spado in Spurs!
Well arm'd Capapee, or for Foot or for Horse;
In his Right he beswagger'd the ready-drawn Sword,
And display'd in his Left th' *invariable Word*:
Like *Dimmock* he challeng'd all 'round with the First,
And prov'd who *resisted*, by T'other, was curst.

Im-

Impreſs'd with true clerical Zeal on his Audience,
Non-Reſiſtance, at length, and Paſſive-Obedience! *

Obj.] Is it thus the learn'd *Pontiff* would have us remember
The Friends of the C*h, and the 4th of *November*?
Thus revive the old Doctrine exploded ſo long;
He but weaken'd the Side which he'd fain have made ſtrong.
*G*e* † needs not ſuch Tenets to eſtabliſh his Throne,
As but an unſatisfied *Stuart* ‡ would own.
Beſides the *Subſcription* he'd like to have marr'd,
As too much in ſubſcribing his Pocket he ſpar'd;
For none wou'd the Foremoſt preſume to ſurpaſs,
The Two Hundred Sterling ſubſcrib'd by his Gr*.

Anſ] Howe'er his Deficience that Way he made good,
By his Preaching, and Praying, and Speeching aloud;
Tho' his Doctrine was odd, and, indeed, obſolete,
Yet his Zeal, Approbation from all of us met.

Pro and *Con* they thus reaſon'd, when in flew a Pigeon,
Special Meſſenger e'er in Affairs of R*l**n;

N 2 On

* See a certain Sermon.
† *Philip*, in the *Spaniſh*.
‡ *Auſtrian*.

On the Wing ſhe coo'd, flutt'ring, as tho' ſhe'd have ſaid,
They had hit, at the laſt, the right Nail on the Head.
The *Congé d'Eliros* went down to elect,
Whom the K* in his Goodneſs was pleas'd to direct;
But the D*n and the C**r, in uſual Pray'r,
Tried first whether Heaven approv'd of th' Affair:
Propitious it prov'd, and inſpir'd them to chuſe
Whom, without *Præmunire*, they durſt not refuſe.
Coercive the Pray'r which makes Heaven ſubmit
To the dictated Terms of his M***y's Writ!
Then they hurried th' *Elect* thro' the Rites of old *B**,
Where, while Conſecration went forward below,
The *Dragon* preſided aloft on the Steeple,
Reproaching the Taſte of our good Chriſtian People.

* *
* * * * * * * * * * * * * * * * * * * *Deſunt multa.*

THE

THE SCANDALIZADE,

A Panegyri-Satiri-Serio-Comi-Dramatic

P O E M.

By *PORCUPINUS PELAGIUS*,
Author of the CAUSIDICADE.

———*Pictoribus atque Poetis*
Quidlibet audendi semper fuit æqua potestas.
HOR.

THE

SCANDALIZADE,

A Panegyri-Satiri-Serio-Comi-Dramatic

POEM.

By PORCUPINUS PELAGIUS,

Author of the CAUSIDICADE.

[illegible]

[illegible]

THE

SCANDALIZADE, &c.

LO! Westward the Church which incumbers the Street,
And is hid by the Shops, so that few People see't,
Which in Virtue of old Dedication belongs
To the sanctify'd Hero renown'd for his *Tongs*,
Whereby, as the Legends of *Britain* disclose,
He fasten'd on *Belzebub's* aqueline Nose,
And held him triumphantly down in the Lurch
'Till he sign'd a *definitive Peace* with the Church.

What

What tho' it its written that *Moor* of *Moor-hall*
Kill'd the *Dragon of Wantley* with nothing at all,
Our Saint has done more, as he gloriously fell
The Dragon's great Master, the Monarch of Hell!
No sooner, however, enlarg'd than to trick us,
As the *French* treats already the Peace of *Sanvicos*,
He set up the *Spirit* to oppose the plain *Letter*,
And so far has got in the Treaty the better.
Alack! that the Saint did not hold him so fast
So as not to escape, or have giv'n him his last.
But that would have utterly ruin'd the Jest,
For where there's no Devil, no need of a Priest.——
But hollo! my Muse, why you straggle too wide,
You're a Mile from your Purpose—Come back for your
Guide:
So the Scribe *del Vagarios* runs heedlessly on
'Till, lost and bewilder'd, he calls out for *St—e*.

On the East of the Church, which opposes the Sun
When first it proclaims that the Day is begun,
Where the ancient *Al-Kibla* within is allow'd,
And religiously reverenc'd still by the Crowd;
There, inwindow'd in Glass, lies a Printseller's Shop,
Where the fam'd Mrs. *Edwards* set formerly up;
(Not she, who incautious, degen'rately wed
The Stains of *Bumbalio*'s contaminate Bed.

Bum-

Bumbalio, *Bumbailiff*, *Bumbroker*, *Bug-Bum*,
Bumbaster, *Bumboaster*, *Hyperbole Tom!*)
Where instead of the Pastrycook's Puddings and Pies
The Sculptor's Impressions catch hold of our Eyes:
There elbowing in 'mong the Crowd with a Jog,
"Lo! good Father *Tobit*, said I, with his Dog!—
But the Artist is wrong; for the Dog should be drawn
At the Heels of his Master in Trot o'er the Lawn."

"To your idle Remarks I take leave to demur,
'Tisn't *Tobit*, nor yet his canonical Cur,
(Quoth a Sage in the Crowd) for I'd have you to know-Sir,
'Tis *Hogarth* himself and his Friend honest *Towser*,
Insep'rate Companions! and therefore you see
Cheek by Joul they are drawn in familiar Degree;
Both striking the Eye with an equal Eclat,
The Bipede *This* here, and the Quadruped *That*——
" You mean—the great Dog and the Man, I suppose,
Or the Man and the Dog—be't just as you chuse."
——You correct yourself rightly—when much to be blam'd,
For the worthiest Person should first have been nam'd.
—Great Dog! why, great Man! methinks you should say,
" Split the Diff'rence, my Friend, they're both great in their Way.

Is't he then so famous for drawing a Punk,
A Harlot, a Rake, and a Parson so drunk,
Whom *Trotplaid* delivers to praise as his Friend,
Thus a Jacknapes a Lion would fain recommend."
The very self same—" how boldly they strike,
And I can't forbear thinking they're somewhat alike."
Oh fie! to a Dog would you *Hogarth* compare?
" No so—I say only they're alike, as it were,
A respectable Pair! all Spectators allow,
And that they deserve an Inscription below
In Capital Letters, *Behold we are Two*."

But, alas! and alack! well-a-day! and so on,
For hardly this Argumentation had done,
E'er a Mutt'ring was heard like the Noise of a Crowd,
Or a Water-Mill Spout,—tho' not quite so loud;
When lo! all the Prints in the Shop seem'd in Action,
Subsiding in Parties,—dividing in Faction,
Promisc'ously adverse, they drew up pell-mell
And pelted each other with Anecdotes well,
While, alternate, to Recriminations they fell.

A ven'rable Set, who set all in a Row,
As some of th' Originals once did for Show,

O'er

O'er *Ulterius Consilium* the Fifth did contend,
Which however went on to a Sixth for an End.
Tho' the three learned *Roberts* would have ſpoke to the
Caſe,
Two Chiefs, and the Third, who deſerv'd the firſt Place;
And the firſt of the Chiefs he had certainly been,
Had the Vacancy fell in the Time of the Queen.

The Firſt both in Law and in Equity read,
O'er a little ſhort Trunk wore a very long Head,
Full equal in every Degree to his Place;
None could better expound or decide on a Caſe,
And yet even fitter, I think, for the MACE.

The Second ſeem'd ſitting as tho' he was doz'd,
And a proud diſpleas'd Look from the Bench he diſ-
clos'd,
But out of his Robe, his ſquare Cap and his Sway,
Altogether the very reverſe every Way,
Good Wit and good Humour, obliging and gay!

The Third, the moſt affable ſure in his Sphere.
Condeſcending and free, genteel, debonair:
He could Buſineſs with Pleaſantry well reconcile,
Unravel with Patience; diſcuſs with a Smile!

In him both the Lawyer and Gentleman met,
And ſeldom together theſe Oppoſites get!
A Judge without Petulance, Av'rice or Haſte,
Whom never the leaſt Imputation diſgrac'd,
Who joy'd with th' Acquitted, and mourn'd with the
Caſt.

Quo', *Niger*, uncouth in his Figure and thin,
A *Jew* all without, yet all *Chriſtian* within,
Such the learn'd Sages who ſat in my Time!——

Talk not of your Days, for they gain'd no Eſteem,
(Cry'd the plauſible Lord in the South of old *Wales*,
Where ſeldom an Yeſterday Comer prevails,)
Except in your Choice of the great Maſter *Tot—ll*,
To ſit by your Side with his Cake and his Rattle.
On a Bench ſomewhat lower, it muſt be confeſt,
You preſided with Honour and rival'd the beſt;
But prompt by Ambition to engroſs the Great *S—l*,
You relinquiſh'd the Poſt where you acted ſo well.
No Man better travell'd the Road than you did,
You hardly once ſtumbled or faulter'd or ſlid;
But when you got out to the open Champain,
Like a Ship, beating rudderleſs over the Main,
You could not the Points of your Compaſs maintain.

Talk

Talk you, resum'd *Niger*, sententiously proud,
Who officiously courted the ill-judging Crowd?
Your Speeches spun ever affectedly fine,
Invariably long and direct like a Line,
Incumber'd with Trappings, superfl'ously vain,
Like *Celia*'s trim Pad when it ambles the Plain.
Tho' Nature did lib'rally well in her Part,
By a clear thinking Head, and perhaps no bad Heart,
Yet 'twas to a Dearth of great Men in your Days,
That you owe, if I reckon aright, all your Praise,
Like Moon-shine unsolid to shine in the Night,
Or a Ghost ever shunning th' Approach of the Light.
O'er thy *Titled-Estate* hangs a black threat'ning Cloud,
Soon ends, says the Scripture, the Name of the Proud,
Lo! the Bastard defrauded, for Justice cries loud!

Then the *Mediterranean* two Heroes engag'd,
Full of Choler and Wrath they alternately rag'd;
Indignantly *This*, in the Swell of his Pride,
And Visage ascaunce, his old Rival decry'd.
Art thou the degenerate Traytor of Hell,
By whose Machinations and Malice I fell,

Who

Who the Fleet and thy King and thy Country betray'd;
Or lagging behind, of the Battle afraid,
Or corrupted abroad, or by Orders from Home,
The Contrivance of *Gentleman Harry* and *Tom*.
To ſlur the great Miniſter's Scheme with Diſgrace,
And to bring their new Converts and Friends into Place,
For that 'tis notorious alone was the Caſe.

Moſt deadly thy Perſon and Name I abhor,
Quo' t'other, as ever I've done heretofore;
That haughty Diſdain, that high Toſs of thy Head,
Or rather that Void on thy Shoulders inſtead,
Might become thee, perhaps, in thy Quarter-deck Strides;
But know, Tyrant, here, thy Topgallant ſubſides!
Superciliouſly ſullen, impatient and vain,
Yet trafficking o'er thy Commiſſion for Gain:
The E—ſt-I-d-a Company this will atteſt,
Who remembers poor *Johnſon* can't fail of the reſt.
Do'ſt aſk if corrupted abroad by the Foe?
Without Heſitation, I anſwer thee, *No!*
If by Orders from Home?—That's nothing to thee.
If prompt by Revenge? known only to me.

Tho'

Tho' my Squadron *came booming*, yet pleas'd I muſt
own,
That I could not arrive 'till I ſaw thee o'erthrown.
But ſay, to what Motive would'ſt have us impute,
Thy arreſting my Squadron ſo cloſe in Purſuit.
The Foe that eſcap'd, I had reach'd and attack'd,
If Jealouſy had not thy Envy awak'd;
Thy Ambition, like Satan's, is far beyond Man,
It's Altitude take no Aſtrolabe can;
Tho' abſolute off of *Toulon* was thy Reign,
Yet at *Deptford* thy Topſail was lower'd amain:
There Juſtice appear'd with her Scales in her Hand,
Thee incapable render'd, me put in Command:
Both weigh'd in the Balance, each Scale in extreme,
Mine prepond'rating low, while thine kick'd the
Beam,
I, Juſtice compelling, thou loſt with the Stream.

Quo' the Third in Command, with his Truncheon
in Hand,
With an Air in his Viſage, half ſurly, half grand,
His Hat, *Khevenhuller*, cock'd up *a-la-mode*,
A *Court-martial* Hero in Sculpture allow'd!
Very happy, unfortunate Chiefs had it been
If the Seas of *Toulen* had but one of you ſeen;

Or

Or rather that both had at *T-b-n* been hang'd,
Then I had prevail'd and the Enemy bang'd;
The two combin'd Fleets had been heard of no more,
Brave *C-nw-ll* had liv'd and the War had been o'er;
No Work had been left to negociate at *Aix*,
Sanvicos had wanted a Name in dispraise;
The Brothers, contented, their Bus'ness had done,
And the Statesman of *St-ff-dshire* never had shone;
His Grace had unpunish'd insulted the Race,
And long Informations had ne'er taken place:
Bronso and *Selim*, *Coalition* great Names!
Hadn't left *Lei'ster-Fields* to make court at St. *James*.
This still had the *Father* continu'd t'abuse,
And the *Son* as betray'd, had not been in the News;
That still had defended th' Apostle St. *Paul*
From imputed Imposture, the Devil and all,
Puff'd *Trotplaid's* iniquitous Son of a Whore,
Tho' partly his own, for the Town to adore.
Tom Jones and St. *P—l!* can a Writer so nice
In his Objects of Virtue, commend to us Vice?
'Tis Nature, forsooth! and must bear a great Price.

Then the Falcon of *Louisbourg* turn'd to the *Hawk*,
Pretend you with me, Brother *Drubber*, to talk?
Tho' your aqueline Beak, your long Talons, and Eyes
Resemble Sir *P-t-r's*, yet reach not their Size;
On

On the Pinions of Glory superior I soar,
On *Europe*'s as well as *America*'s Shore;
I invaded *Cape-Breton*, and beat off the Foe,
Came home, and so gave them another good Blow;
And had giv'n them a Third hadn't you stept between:
Methinks, you have manag'd but oddly your Scene;
With a Force much superior you hardly could beat,
You *drubb'd* them, 'tis true, but it was not complete,
You suffer'd the *Admiral*'s Ship to retreat.

Say you so, quo' the *Hawk?* prithee, Friend, let me know,
What's become of your much-boasted Victory now?
Where's now your *Cape-Breton*, forsooth! and your Isle?
Why restor'd to the Foe, as hardly worth while.
For the beardless *Sanvicos*, be't said to his Praise,
Gave it up, as worth nothing, to close up at *Aix*.
The other Adventure can't well be call'd yours,
That, Fame to your mighty Commander secures;
By him each Transaction and Matter was done;
'Twas he that did ev'ry great Action *alone*;
For has he not wrote in his Letter, *'Twas I*
Did this, and did that:—can an *Admiral* lie?

For it was not his Fault that he lagg'd in the Rear,
And that all Things were over before he came there;
But his Ship mov'd delib'rately on like a Snail,
And would not, on Sight of the Battle, make ſail.
Then plume not yourſelf in another Man's Robe,
Nor vie with Lord *Tar*, who has rounded the Globe,
And, thirſting for P—age, wiſh'd for juſt ſuch a Jobb.

What's that you advance, quo' the Man in the O?
Of the World emblematic, he paſs'd to and fro;
In a *Spencer* as gay as a Boy in his Geers,
But in Looks as much beaten by Weather and Years.
You ſo fam'd there, cry'd he, in the Mouth of each Fellow,
For taking, with *Six* Men of War, *Porto Bello*;
Whoſe Birth-day, forſooth! was obſerv'd with ſuch Joys,
Such Rantings, ſuch Roarings, ſuch Bonfires and Noiſe!
Whoſe Head hangs aloft, as a Sign ev'ry where,
To warn in the Porter to *Calvert*'s Butt Beer;
Who alarm'd all the Coaſt with the Coming of *Ned*,
And frighten'd our *two Brother-Stateſmen* in Bed;
Who wrote, and who printed, and publiſh'd ſuch Letters,
As were not ſo fit to be read of your Betters;

Abus'd

Abus'd and insulted us all at the *Board*:
You are broke, and cashier'd, and will ne'er be re-
ſtor'd.
Very few, like myſelf, make a Quarter-deck Lord!

Is it ſo, my fine Lord, *Accapult*-Buccaneer?
The old Sailor reply'd, with a kind of a Sneer;
Unvers'd in the Art and the Miſt'ry of Sail,
Or to take, of a Voyage, a faithful Detail;
By th' Aſſiſtance of Agents thou'ſt compaſs'd the Ball,
Experienc'd Lieutenants are ready at Call.
By Chance and good Fortune you hit on a Ship,
Which however had like to have giv'n you a Slip;
By Chance 'twas you rounded the Point of *Cape-Horn*,
By Chance you diſcover'd the Iſland forlorn,
By Chance you eſcap'd being taken to *France*,
To learn the fine Shrug *a-la-mode*, and to dance,
And all your Succeſs was the Work of mere Chance!

Art thou the bold Hero, the Fav'rite of Fame,
Who with only five Servants to *Caledon* came,
Yet grew to an Army ſo num'rous and ſtrong,
That frighten'd our run-away Gen'rals along?
This ſurpriz'd at the *Pans*, you ſoon made to run,
To apprize all he met with, the Fight was begun.

That, the hardy black Tyrant of Discipline's Force!
You taught to confide in the Heels of his Horse;
Then advanc'd into *England* o'er good Mother *W*—;
Very fit to command was a Man so decay'd!
Scour'd round all the Country along up to *D—y*,
'Till you heard at the Head of my Troops I was hard-
by;
When, wisely returning, you shunn'd future Harms,
To revel in fair *Jenny Cameron*'s Charms,
'Till we met at *Culloden* in opposite Arms!

Art thou the more famous great Hero, who did
Pursue me so close at the Heel o'er the *Tweed*,
Cross'd over the *Spey*, and fell all on a sudden,
So furiously on in the Plains of *Culloden*?
Where, as *Jacobites* tell us, you flew o'er the Slain,
Rekindled the Slaughter'd to kill o'er again,
Where all the old Women throughout that old Realm,
Old Women there are, besides those at your Helm;
Pronounc'd you should gain never Victory more,
And that *Saxe* should revenge me of *Jacobite* Gore;
But what need you care, you have got your Reward,
It's Magnitude shews how some People fear'd!
A Reward! which perpetuates jointly our Names,
The terrible Frights which I rais'd at St. *J*—!

Great

Great Danger enlarges for ever the Soul,
And who gives in his Fright always gives like a Fool.
Now Peace is proclaim'd, and that false *Louis Quinze*,
Having done his own Business, my Int'rest declines,
I am order'd to wait on the *Pope* and my Sire,
While you to the Shades of sweet *Windsor* retire,
From the Hurry and Noise of the City remote,
Your Cares in the Arms of a Fair one forgot,
The Bum-bailiff's Daughter, or cleanly *Marmot*.

The King of the Island far out in the Seas,
Directly in Front of the false *Genoese*,
His Body in Armour, his Head in a Wig,
Strange Dress for a Camp, prepost'rously big!
His Mien discompos'd, and his Eyes in a Fright,
As when the bold *Koningsegg* storm'd him at Night;
When, with *Broglio*, oblig'd to desert his Command,
This in Night-gown and Slippers—That with Breeches
in Hand.
Quo' he, you may compliment, Sirs, as you please;
Perhaps I myself may cross over the Seas.
For if it be true, what some People advance,
Tho' credited little with us or in *France*,
That the *Trowel* begot the Male Child on the *Pan*,
Where's the Casuist? where the Civilian that can
Deny to my Face that I am not the Man?

That,

That, reſponſive the Monarch *Borruſian*, will I
With very good Arguments flatly deny.
That Proteſtant Iſle, as well you as I-know,
Reject the Abſurdity *Jure Divino.*
That the many is made for one Man they diſown;
But the Man for the many, tho' born to a Crown!
And therefore, retaining ſome Pow'r in their Hands,
Their Kings are not abſolute in their Commands,
They are bound within Laws, beyond which they can't go,
Excepting to *H——r* only,——or ſo.
I've a Right in Remainder, and therefore inſiſt,
Hereditary Right is, no more than a Jeſt:
The Poſſeſſor, you know, will eſtabliſh his Throne,
You've heard, 'gainſt what Father 'twas done by the Son;
The Sire would reſume, but he could not prevail,
Too late he found out he had Cauſe to bewail,
The Son on the Throne, and the Father in Jail!

Quo' *Gallus*, Great Grandſon of old *Mazarine*,
Who begot the perfidious *Le-Grand* on the Queen,
Would you ſeek out a Sceptre where Parliaments ſway,
Where the M—y govern, and Monarchs obey?

To

To be forc'd, upon ev'ry Occasion to bribe
An abandon'd, corrupt, most untractable Tribe,
Averse to their Duty! like *Crassus* of old,
Or modern * * *, devoted to Gold.
A profligate Nation, full ripe for the Chain,
Where they sell off themselves to be sold o'er again.
A People, as one of their Poets well says,
No Monarch could govern, or God could e'er please!
Where the Sov'reign is kept by a Faction in durance,
And *Two Brothers* govern by dint of Assurance;
But why, my good Friend, and my Pupil of *France*,
Who taught you the Nicety of Complaisance;
To prevaricate likewise, and trick *a-la-mode*,
With Men upon Earth, and in Heaven with God;
Why, I say, so severe on *Emanuel*'s Sore,
Now our own in Alliance by Marriage Pow'r?
Suppose, in Reply, he'd retorted the Blame,
Your undutiful Plot, and your run-away Scheme,
From your Country, your Father, your Home and your King,
The confed'rate Lieutenants sad Fate in a String!
Whosoe'er has deserv'd or the Halter or Block,
Should be cautious of mentioning either, or mock,
But there be, who are known to've a very good Stock.

Cleopatra,

Cleopatra, theſe Kings, quo' *Juliet*, talk all,
We Queens can't put in for a Toſs at the Ball;
They may ſay what they pleaſe of their Sceptres and
Pow'r,
We can humble them down in the Eighth of an Hour;
We ſubdue not to kill in their butcherly Way,
Embraces our Weapons, our Battles but Play.
Superior you are, I muſt own, in your Fame,
Great-Britain and *Ireland* your Conqueſts proclaim;
With powerful Art you diſplay your wide Shield,
And take in, by Turns, ev'ry Spear in the Field;
Whole Troops you take Pris'ners, and gloriouſly dare,
While only one Captive can fall to my Share;
One ſingle Companion is all that I claim,
Like the Turtle, with him, in the Deſart I am,
Or the Parable Prophet's poor Man with his Lamb.

In anſwer, retorted the Tragedy-Queen,
Not leſs than myſelf are you virtuous, I ween,
This Diff'rence, however, between us there be,
You're the Right of another, while I am quite free;
What e'er you're poſſeſs'd of is Matter of Truſt,
You've Accounts with your Huſband to ſtate and ad-
juſt;

While

While I, unembarras'd with Master or Spouse,
Can neither the one or the other abuse:
Incapable therefore of raising the Horn,
I range thro' the World; for Confinement I scorn.
But wherefore, in different Attitudes here,
You thus, in the Guise of two Persons appear,
As tho' you had meant, that the Sculptor should mend,
By practising various, his Hand in the End:
Or did the two Rivals endeavour t'excel?
The Spouse drew you ugly, the Keeper a *Belle!*
But if I judge right, by th' Extent of your Mouth,
They need not have quarrell'd, there's room for them both;
To the dark Shade of *Tartarus*, wide is the Gate,
But that to *Elysium* is narrow and strait,
Alternate Possession is not a bad State.

That's a Touch, quo' *Mac Flora*, on you, my dear *Con*,
For two Mezatinto's of you have been done;
You thought that the first was not handsome enough,
And therefore condemn'd it as pitiful Stuff:
You publish'd it bore no Resemblance to Truth,
And was rather more like to wild *Peter* the Youth,
Again must the Sculptor attempt an Essay,
And give to *September* the Charms of sweet *May*.

He has curiously done it, and if it be true,
A fairer there's none, or a lovelier than you;
To gain such a Beauty, who would not deceive?
But the Wonder is rather, how the De'il one could leave.
Strange! you held not in Spousal, for better for worse,
Save one Ingrate only, half Mule and half Horse,
A Trader in Beauty, a Broker in Love,
A BATAVIAN alone from your Side could remove;
From thy sorrowful Lines he'll no Honor receive,
The stigmatiz'd *Tartuff* there also will live,
While all reading Maidens learn Caution and grieve.

You squeeze up your Mouth, Madam *Flora*, so tight,
Well the Men are appriz'd what is signify'd by't;
Assignations of Love you'll disdain, I suppose,
One only except with the Lilly *White Rose*.
While him o'er the Mountains you carefully led,
The Heath on Occasion——might have made a good Bed.
That I judge, I must own, by myself in the Case,
Had he found what I lost, when they ript up my Lace,
My Hero! my Sov'reign! brave King of the Fair!
More especially those who unfortunate are,

I had

I had not been left to appeal to the Town,
Againſt Injuries hardly before never known,
To any, myſelf but excepted alone.

Damn the B-t-s, quo' *Quin*, in his Sir *John Brute* Tone,
Or rather, which ſtill is more brutiſh, his own;
What means theſe two Players: Blood and Ooons, with a Pox;
This here caſting downwards intenſly her Looks;
That diſcloſing her tempting Protub'rance of Breaſt,
Which calls for the Hand, and invites to the Feaſt.
But yet to acknowledge the Truth on their Part,
The Copies are far of th' Originals ſhort.
But *Garrick*, thou little proud Imp of the Stage,
I laugh when I ſee thee in *Lilliput* rage,
In Comedy ever a Fribble or Toy,
A *Lothario* in Buſkin, or Hobble-de-hoy.
For the Sculptor's Impreſſion what is thy Deſert?
Like a Taylor on Sunday, ſo trim and ſo pert!
Yet, forſooth? the true Figure of *Richard* muſt be
Shewn in thee to the Public, as well as in me.
But as well may a *Jack'napes* be ſhewn for a Man,
Or a draggle-tail Goſling contend with a Swan,

As thou ſhould'ſt, in vain Competition, preſume,
To rival Great *Quin* in the Buſkin and Plume,
In the Monarchs of *Britain*, or th' Heroes of *Rome.*

What, *Garrick* reply'd, is thy Claim to a Print?
Is't to ſhew to the World how ſurly thou'rt in't?
In Sir *John* and ſuch Parts, thou'ſt a natural Brawl,
Who ſees thee in theſe, ſees thee acting in all;
Thy Voice a monotonous Cadence imparts,
Too ſparing thy Actions, and thoſe but by Starts;
Sometimes ill-adapted, as if in a Huff,
Thou art punching thy Belly, or ſtripping to Buff.
As well in compare may the Brewer's Dray-Horſe
Be ſet 'gainſt a Racer which ſkips o'er the Courſe,
As thou, my good Friend, be oppos'd againſt me,
In the Wiles of King *Richard* ſo boaſted by thee
In *Othello* or *Lear*, diſtinguiſhing Three!

Lo! old Captain *Coram*, ſo round in the Face,
And a Pair of good Chops plumpt up in good Caſe,
His amiable Locks hanging grey either Side
To his double-breaſt Coat o'er his Shoulders ſo wide.
Malcontented, he cry'd, 'tis with Sorrow I ſee
A Scheme made a Job of, projected by me.

This

This ſame *Nova Scotia* will hardly ſucceed
To provide for a Lobſter abroad was the Deed,
Boundry Commiſſi'ners, and Agents, and Clerks,
Loungers, and Leaches, and ſuch kind of Sharks.

Then Architect *Biggs*, ſo lumb'ringly full,
Like the Church he erected, expenſively dull.
Addreſs'd the old Captain; prithee why doſt thou ſob?
Nova Scotia's in very good Hands for a Jobb:
For is not the Government civil forſooth!
With all its free Laws, in the Governor's Mouth?
But this is not all the Effect of thy Pains,
The *Hoſpital Foundling* came out of thy Brains.
To encourage the Progreſs of vulgar Amours
The breeding of Rogues and th' increaſing of Whores,
While the Children of honeſt good Huſbands and Wives
Stand expos'd to Oppreſſion and Want all their Lives.
Was it conſcious of revelling erſt in the Sport,
That hath prompted thee thus to deprecate for't?
For, methinks, I can ſtill in thy Countenance ſee,
Thou haſt many a Laſs grappl'd under the Lee;
But thou'rt in thy Projects ſo wondrouſly nice,
Thou quit'ſt them as ſoon as they're ſet to a Price,
So teſtily honeſt thou art in thy Choice.

Quo'

Quo' the golden-ear'd *Ricard* to Patriot *Bernardo*,
A powerful Alderman each in his Ward-O!
Methinks, you look bigger in Print than in Stone,
Here larger than at the Exchange you are done,
Where the Merchants admiring gape fervently at-you,
And hope to be hewn out likewise into Statue.
What Honour from Portraits can Citizens claim,
While Players can draw from the Sculptor the same;
From the Fields of old *Goodman* you chas'd them away,
As they ruin'd our 'Prentices all by their Play.
But pray, Brother Cit, is it true that you trim?
'Tis said you're a *Pellamite* up to the Brim.
That you've help'd them to Cash is a very plain Case,
Your Scheme for reducing the Int'rest takes Place;
And if there is Truth in the public Report,
Your Friends are preferr'd in the Camp and in Court.
That you've loudly declar'd for the Peace, it is true,
And rival in Brok'rage proud *Gideon* the Jew;
Is this your Attachment to long-headed *John*?
How soon you've forgot the fair Sov'reign of *Hun*!
What was anciently said by the Scholar True still-is,
Tempora mutantur & nos mutamur in illis.

Indeed,

Indeed, Brother Alderman, that you're a Cit,
Quo' the ſober *Bernardo*, appears by your Wit.
'Tis true, for the Peace I did loudly declare,
Becauſe the *Two Brothers* knew nothing of War.
That I help'd them to Money is likewiſe as true,
Unwilling my Country ſhould ſink in my View.
Oft my *Yea* among thoſe of the Court did appear,
But 'twas to defray the Supplies of the Year;
Still with long-headed *John* are my Heart and my
Hand,
And the fair Queen of *Hun* may my Service command.
But when blundering Pilots have ſeiz'd on the Helm,
With their Ears full of Wool, on their Eyeballs a
Film.
I muſt not lie bye unconcern'd in the Ship,
And not lend a hand when ſhe ſinks in the deep,
Like the Paſſenger erſt, or *Jonas* aſleep.

Then *Colley* cry'd out to *Mac Swiny*, Hah! Friend,
Stop my Vitals, I'm glad you're ſo far from your End;
Once Patron of Wit, of the Buſkin and Stage,
Diſengag'd in your Mien, unincumber'd your Age.
Your reſpectable Head cover'd o'er with white Hairs,
Your Face full and open, unwrinkl'd with Cares,

Un-

Unconcern'd you ſit looking about in your Chair,
And lift the white Beaver aloft with an Air,
As tho', in your Age, you would ſet up to dare.

What, ſtill, my Friend *Colley*, in plenary Bronze,
Which grac'd, anſwer'd *Swiny*, my Company once;
Tho' early thy *Proff'rings* conſpicuouſly ſhone,
And thy uſual *Outdoings* were never outdone.
Very ſtrange Apprehenſions ſtill haunted my Hope,
As ſome Prognoſtications methought of a Rope
Diſclos'd in thy Looks; but I'm wond'rouſly glad
I'm deceiv'd in th' unlucky Opinion I had;
Tho' all muſt allow thou'rt a Genius for Play,
In Tragedy ſolemn, in Comedy gay;
An excellent Judge of the Drama and Scene,
Beyond what theſe Times have ever yet ſeen;
An Original both off the Stage, and upon,
Heav'n ſend that thy Fate mayn't devolve on thy Son!
Yet how haſt thou chanc'd on a Call into Court,
To drink up the Sack ſo unqualify'd for't?
Thou'ſt worn quite down to the Stumps *Joyous Morn*,
And the Crambo reſponſive of *Great Cæſar born!*
Thou ſeem'ſt to denote of Ideas a Dearth;
But I ſee thou'rt inclining to old Parent Earth,

Thy

Thy Fame, in Appeal, to Posterity yielding,
Thy Bronze to thy Son, and thy Lawrel to *F—d—g*,
That Fame, as an Author, so long in the Building.

Hoa! there, to whom none can, forsooth, hold a Candle,
Call'd the lovely-fac'd *Heidegger* out to *George H-d-l*;
In arranging the Poets sweet Lines to a Tune,
Such as, *God save the King*, or the fam'd *Tenth of June*.
How amply your Corpulence fills up the Chair?
Like mine Host at an Inn, or a *London* Lord-May'r,
Three Yards, at the least, round about in the Waist,
In Dimensions your Face like the Sun in the West;
But a Chine of good Pork, and a Brace of good Fowls,
A dozen-pound Turbut, and two Pair of Soals,
With Bread in Proportion devour'd at a Meal,
How incredibly strange, and how monstrous to tell!
Needs must that your Gains and your Income be large,
To support such a vast *unsupportable* Charge!
Retrench, or e'er long you may set your own Dirge.

Thou Perfection, as far as e'er Nature could run,
Of the ugly, quo' *H--d--l*, in th' ugliest Baboon,
Human Nature, and even thy Maker's Disgrace,
So frightful thy Looks, so grotesc is thy Face!
With a Hundred deep Wrinkles impress'd on thy Front,
Like a Map with a great many Rivers upon't.
Thy lascivious Ridotto's, obscene Masquerades,
Have unmaided whole Scores ev'ry Season of Maids.
Would'st upbraid with Ill-nature as monstrous and vast,
My moderate Eating, and delicate Taste,
When I paid but Two Hundred a Year for my Board;
True, my Landlord soon after the Bargain deplor'd;
Withdrew, became Bankrupt, a Prey to the Law,
His Effects swallow'd up in disputing a Flaw,
'Mong Councel, Attornies, Commissi'ners and such,
And all the long Train so accustom'd to touch.
But what is this Matter of Bankrupt to me,
All Folks must abide by the Terms they agree,
If guilty my Stomach, my Conscience is free.

The mendicant Son of the pious St. *Francis*,
Grown pale o'er the Lamp and religious Romances,
With Mortification inscrib'd in his Looks;
In his Hand swung a Basket of Scraps from the Cooks

For

For the Use of the Convent, while yet for his own,
On his Back in a Wheat-sheaf he carried a Nun.
Hold, quo' he, Brother Flogger, astride of the Fair,
With her lovely Posteriors expos'd to the Air,
Deface not that delicate Prospect with Wounds,
Spare that lilly-white Pair of delightful Half-rounds;
Say, barbarous Man, what's the Meaning of this?
How can you chastise, where you rather should kiss,
The Verge of the Court ever privileg'd is.

Brother, answer'd the Flogger, 'tis not for the Sin,
But because I've found out where a Rival has been;
Lo! I'm not so severe, my Scourge is of Furrs,
'Tis the Tail of a Fox I apply thus to hers;
My Heart, I must own, does my Stripes countermand,
More in earnest my Eyes are employ'd than my Hand;
But hah! my good Brother, what's that I discern?
A Pair of bright Eyes peeping out thro' your Corn;
A Pair of long Heels too, and fine pointed Toes,
The Feet of a Woman, by G-d, or her Shoes!
Say our Order, ah! Brother, whatever it will
Nature's oppos'd by Restriction but ill;
There is in a Woman a *natural Cause*,
Like a Magnet the *Needle* it pow'rfully draws,

True, her Abſence does mortify much to our Coſt;
But 'tis too much of Woman that mortifies moſt,
Very numerous they who are loſt on that Coaſt.

The two next that began at each other to lour,
Was Preſbyter *Tom* and his Gr—. of *Cantaur*:
Each fam'd in his Way, was much reckon'd upon,
This Prime of th' *eſtabliſh'd*, and that of *Non-con!*
Whoſe rev'rend good Looks and ven'rable Hairs,
Concur in diſplaying near Seventy Years.
Hairs! white as the band ſpreading under his Chin,
Or his Innocence dwelling, all conſcious, within.
Plain was his Garb, like the Doctrine he taught,
But not without Seam, as his Maſter's was wrought,
With the Church he ſtood well, but was ſtrong againſt Tithe,
In Company eaſy, and decently blithe.
Never angry, unleſs that an Oath ſhould have flown,
Or that any aſſerted that Three was not One.
Quo' he, my good Lord, you look wond'rouſly great,
With your Furbeloes round, and your Flounces in pleat,
Your Silks and your Lawns, and your Black and your white!
But, methinks you appear diſcompos'd with a Fright;
Your

Your Eyes look aghaſt with a horrible Glare,
Like *Garrick*, in *Richard* of *England*, you ſtare!
As tho' that th' *Italian* Advent'rer was come,
At the Head of his Rebels with Bagpipe and Drum.
Ill the Wind, quo' the Adage, which Good to none blew,
What has hang'd up ſo many, has dignify'd you;
For it's very well known, but for that bloody Work,
You ſtill had remain'd Father Pr-m-te of *Y*—.
That you've well done your Duty it muſt be confeſs'd,
You fought like a Soldier, and pray'd like a Prieſt,
Jack-boots be your Arms, and a Sabre your Creſt!

Tho' Foe, quoth his G—, to Church Tithes and to Dues,
You never a moderate Off'ring refuſe;
You're as deep, in effect, as ourſelves, in the Mire,
Tho' the Form you reject, you accept of the Hire.
If my Robe is incumb'ring, your Coat tho' ſo plain,
Bears a Cut *a-la-mode*, and is therefore profane.
Be't ſo that we two be Philoſopher-like,
If you at my Robes like *Diogenes* kick,
You'll allow that, like *Plato*, I likewiſe may chide,
And ſay your plain Coat may contain as much Pride.
Come, come, Brother Prieſt, let's walk Side by Side.

Then

Then old *Æsculapius*, in Physic a Sage,
A very good Figure, consid'ring his Age!
Sometimes out of Fashion, sometimes again in,
For so, as Occasion occurr'd, has he been.
Pourtray'd very gracefully grand in his Chair,
Much esteem'd by the Men, much *chastiz'd* by the
Fair.
But you, *Pill-man*, you *Drop-man*, you *Nostrum-man*,
there,
With all your sham Patients, how stiff you appear?
Pray what's the Ingredient that makes up your Pill?
How dare you prescribe without Knowledge to kill?
These may perhaps instance the Cures you have made,
But where are all those who've been lost by your Trade?

The Namesake, replying, of the Son of old *Nun*,
An Astronomer vast, who arrested the Sun!
The System of Physic was first like a Wood,
One could not get thro' for the Branches that stood,
'Till the Doctors *Hippocrates*, *Galen*, and more,
Cut their Passage quite thro' and left open the Door.
He's a Doctor of course who keeps in the Track,
But if he successfully deviates, a Quack;

He

He is *rectus in curia* who murders by Rule,
But who cures by the bye is a dangerous Fool.
You exclaim at my *Nostrum*, because it is so,
You should not condemn an Affair you don't know;
You may, learnedly dull, be obedient to rule,
Attend to the Pulse and inspect the Close-stool,
Prescribe in corrupt Combination with Shops,
And surfeit your Patients with nauseating Slops,
My *Drop* I'll administer, guiltless, or Pill,
And as few as the least of the Faculty kill.
What is it to me what the Faculty blames?
Lo! *M-t-m-r*'s censur'd, as likewise is *J——*;
Both these in the Arms of *Hippocrates* bred;
Large Volumes the last hath both written and read,
And prithee, what Doctor among you so clever?
He cures with a Mouthful of Powder a Fever.

Lo! sweet Lady *Peace*, so dispos'd at her Ease
Sanvitos's Daughter, begotten at *Aix*,
Definitive Madam! I'll sing you a Song,
For it seems your *Definity* will not last long,
With your Olive, quo' *Barb*, in your Lilly-white
Hand;
In the other a Rapier quite out of Command:

That

That very ſame Rapier we humbly preſume,
Which fought ſo abroad, and was loſt ſo at home;
Which, ſcorning to run with its Maſter away,
Slipt off from his Side, and was left in the Fray.
With its Point to the Ground it now uſeleſs reclines
'Till the War is rekindled by good *Louis Quinze.*

Is it you, anſwer'd ſhe, with his Sonnets and Catches,
Your Cavalier Air and your Hand in your Breeches?
Your Bawble-ſtring dangling a-down with a Knob,
To ſhew you've a *Pinchbeck* that lurks in your Fob.
You, forſooth! muſt a Lady of Quality wed,
Say, how did her Quality reliſh in Bed?
And which of you two did moſt ſtupidly err,
She in marrying thee, or thou marrying her?
But finely embroider'd, indeed, is your Veſt,
Lo! a Beau of fine Taſte ev'ry Way, I proteſt!
A Face not ill form'd, had it not been ſo round,
An infallible Mark you're but mod'rately crown'd,
Like moſt of your Brethren, the Lovers of Sound.
Then a Voice quite unknown, cry'd out, Candidate *Van*,
Beware! the *High-B—h—f* turns Cat in the Pan.

But

But methinks, you owe more for your Form and your Feature
To your Maker in Sculpture, than your Maker in Nature,
Whom the clamorous Sons of the Bones and the Clever,
Cry up with a *Vandepotijah* for ever!
Well turn'd in your Person, genteel in your Mien,
Or so by my Lady, at least, you were seen.
Two *Sosia's!* i'faith, as in *Dryden* or *Plautus*,
Master *Ridley* has varied what *Knapton* had brought us.
Rivals contending for Fame in the Charge,
This here gives a *V-nd—t*, that a Sir G—;
Both with one Hand *negligé* in the Breast,
As tho' you were sure of th' Election confest,
The other extended, as tho' to receive
The kind Contributions th' Electors may give:
Of the Quarrels regardless, the Flouts and the Fleers,
And the Challenges eke of the two Scrutineers,
As if the bad Voters were all on Behalf,
Of *Tear'em*, the Son of old *Gore'um* of *Staff*.
But the Sculptors have vied in a delicate Taste,
And even great *Tamerlain*'s Painter surpass'd,
In covering the little Defect of the *Cast*.

The studious Philosopher waking at once,
As out of the Depth of a very deep Trance,
Unclenching his Fingers and scrubbing his Pate,
All bare, and close shav'd, without Perr'wig or Hat.
Staring frighted around him, and raising his Voice,
Cry'd out, what a Devil d'ye mean by this Noise?
I'd the Longitude fast in my Ken making out;
In three Minutes more I had done it no doubt,
Had I not been disturb'd in the Thread of my Thought,
Which just to the Point of Perfection was brought.
As a Fowler who's gotten the Game in his Eye,
And presenting his Piece, is about to let fly,
Alarm'd by the Dogs in the Wood, in a Fright,
It takes to the Wing and is soon out of Sight;
So I—ah! farewel Thirty Thousand good Pounds,
The Reward of the Parliament!——Ad's Blood and
Ounds!

But above, the two Savages, beating the Hour,
The deliberate Clock sounded Twelve, and no more,
The Charm was dissolv'd, and the Prints lost their
Power.

The K E Y.

PAGE 95. St. *Dunstan's* Church.

96. *Sanvicos, S--d--ch.*

del Vagarios, N--c--le.

Bumbalio, Auctioneer *J-nes.*

98. l. 3. *Trotplaid, F--ld--ng.*

99. l. 3. *R. Raymond. R. Eyre. R. Price.*

100. *Niger,* L-d Ch--ll-r *K--g.*

l. 10. L-d Ch--ll-r *T-lb-t.*

101. l. 13. Here hangs a Tale.

l. 18. Ad--l *M-th--s.*

102. l. 4. The Two Brothers.

l. 9. *L-st--ck.*

104. l. 4. The brave Captain *Cornwall.*

l. 8. L-d *G--r.*

l. 11. *Bronso* and *Selim, P--t* and *L-t-lt-n.*

l. 13. The K--g.

l. 14. The P--ce.

l. 22. Ad--l *W--n.*

l. 23. *H--k.*

106. l. 8. and 10. L-d *A-s-n.*

l. 13. Ad--l *V-r--n.*

107. l. 17. Young Che-l--r.

l. 20. *C-pe* and *H--l-y.*

108. l. 10. D-- of *C--b--l---d.*

109. l. 10. K--g of *S-rd--a.*
110. l. 1. K--g of *P--ſ-a.*
l. 18. K--g of *F--ce.*
111. l. 15. K--g of *S-rd--a.*
112. l. 1. Mrs. *W-f-gton* and Mrs. *C-bb-r.*
113. l. 16. *Con. Ph--l-ps.*
114. l. 6. *M-ilm-n.*
118. l. 1. *H-re* and *B-rn-rd.*
119. l. 9. L--d *Gr-nv-le.*
122. l. 2. *H--del.*
124. l. 5. Mr. *B-db-ry* and the A-ch-B--p.
126. l. 1. *M--d.*
l. 13. *W-rd.*
127. l. 21. *B--rd.*

THE

THE PASQUINADE.

WITH NOTES VARIORUM.

BOOK the FIRST.

Ay, 'tis a Cruſt, a laſting Cruſt for the Rogues, I would be glad to ſee the proudeſt of them all but dare to nibble at this,—if they do, it will rub their Gums for them I promiſe you.

BAYES.

THE

PASQUINADE.

WITH

NOTES VARIORUM.

BOOK the FIRST.

Ay, but a Critick [illegible] ... dare to [illegible] ... their Guns for them I promise you.

BAYES.

THE

PASQUINADE.

BOOK the FIRST.

O Chief in Verse! O ev'ry Muses' Care!
Pride of each mortal and immortal Fair!
Whether

ANNOTATIONS.

Pasquinade.] As it is highly necessary that every Writer, who publishes his Works for the Instruction and Emolument of the Publick, should write in such a Manner as to be understood by those of a common Capacity, as well as by those, who, as the Poet says,

——Peruse a Work of Wit
With the same Spirit that its Author writ;

Or,

Whether enraptur'd with *Urania*'s Charms,
Or sunk in *Chloe*, or *Amanda*'s Arms;

Whe-

ANNOTATIONS.

Or, if he does not, as it is highly becoming the Scholiast to make them familiar to such Readers, I should think myself very unworthy to illustrate the following Poem, did I pass over the *Name* itself; which, tho' some Critics may understand, I am persuaded many do not.——Know then, that *Pasquin* was a *Cobler*, who work'd in his Stall at *Rome*; about the Beginning of the fifteenth Century; and, being a Fellow of ready Wit and a satyrical Disposition, the People flock'd about him to hear him rally and talk Politics, at which he was very expert. After his Decease, the Statue of a Gladiator being dug up near his Stall, it was set up and call'd *Pasquin*; the *Wits*, his Pupils, taking it in their Heads, in honour to their *dead* Master, to stick their Lampoons, Satires, and Libels thereon; all which were termed *Pasquinades*. If thou doubted, Reader, whether this Poem was ever hung on the said Statue, if thou take a Walk to a certain Corner of the Palace of *Ursines* in *Rome*, thou may'st enquire further concerning it.

Line 1. *O thief in Verse.*] The great Personage here addressed, from what we may gather from the following Lines, can be no other than Dr. *John Hill*, *Acad. Rege Scient. Burd.* &c. *Soc.* and *Inspector General* of *Great Britain*.

Lines 3, 4. *Whether enraptur'd*, &c.] These Lines seem to hint at the Amours of Mr. *Inspector*, ho has so often celebrated, in his Works, his *Chloes*, *Daphnes*, and *Amandas*, all Ladies of Quality, whose Favours, some have been bold enough to say, have been of the same Nature with those he

received

Whether eternal Bays thy Temples grace,
Or thy lac'd *night-cap* well supplies their Place;
Whether with *Goddess*, or with earthly *Qual*,
You saunter down *Parnassus*, or the *Mal*;
Or, in Philosophy profoundly wise,
You pore intent with microscopic Eyes,

New

ANNOTATIONS.

received from the Muses; purely imaginary; but we presume not to assert this Opinion, 'till we have some Authority to suppose those Ladies as chaste as the Sisters of *Parnassus*.

Line 6. *Or thy lac'd Night-cap.*] A Night-cap, ornamented with *Brussels* Lace, which this Enamorato used to wear on particular Occasions, when honour'd in the Embraces of *Quality*. ANON:

Line 8. *You saunter down.*] Alluding to a *Je ne scais quoi* in the Carriage of this Gentleman, by some virulent Writers, called an *indolent Waddle*, by others, *a janty Air.*——Vide *Libitina sine conflictu, Woodward's Letter, &c.*

Line 10. *You pore intent with microscopic Eyes.*] From the Contradiction this Passage seems to imply to that of another great Author and Philosopher, who says,

Why has not Man a microscopic Eye?

It might possibly be concluded that some Mistake had happened, either in transcribing or printing this Line; and that our Author intended it, *thro' microscopic Eyes*, meaning the Eyes, or the Glasses of his Microscope: But, if any Credit

New Worlds discover in a *Catharine Pear*,
Or Monsters animate in sour small Beer,

Serenely

ANNOTATIONS.

may be given to this Gentleman's Discoveries in Natural Philosophy, we must conclude he himself is possess'd of Eyes infinitely more discerning than the rest of the Virtuosi; having found out such Animalculæ, and their Method of Existence, as no other Philosopher ever did, or ever will, though assisted by all the Helps of the most improved Microscope, unless possess'd of the same Kind of Eyes: The visual Rays to which are so ductile, that they not only are directed from real Objects, but from *no* Objects at all,——which Accomplishment alone should sufficiently establish this great Man as the Prince of Philosophers, and empower him to correct and censure the Researches of others: As we must own the Eye that can *see* what is *invisible*, is certainly more able to explore the Secrets of Nature, than that which can see only *what is to be seen*.——I find no Reason therefore to vary the Reading in the Text.

Line 11. *New Worlds discover in a Catharine Pear.*] Among the philosophic Researches hinted in the preceding Annotation, take the following, made by this Gentleman on a rotten Pear.——

" It was but a very small Portion of the covered Surface " of the Pear that could be brought within the Area of the " Microscope, but this appeared, under its Influence, a wide " Extent of Territory: varied with Hills and Lawns, with " winding Hollows, open Plains, and shadowy Thickets." Inspector.

A very

Serenely trace their *fundamental Breath*,
Whilſt thy grim Lion grinds thy Foes to Death :

O let

ANNOTATIONS.

A very material Objection indeed ariſes againſt our Author, in reſpect that he calls it a *Catharine Pear*; as this Philoſopher in his Preamble to the Experiment, expreſsly ſays, it was a *French* Pear, in which we cannot think him miſtaken, as he took ſuch particular Notice of the ſaid Pear; for, ſays he, it was cut by a Perſon very fond of Pears, who out of that exceſſive Fondneſs eat a thin Slice, and reſerved the reſt to another Opportunity: That he cried *Pah!* at ſeeing it again when rotten, and that it was cut at the largeſt End.— *Vide Inſpector* 332. So that from theſe Circumſtances, we muſt remark this as an Error in our Author.

Line 13. *Fundamental Breath.*] Alluding to an Animal, which this profound Enquirer into Nature diſcover'd, whoſe Organs of Reſpiration are ſituated in its Fundament; and which continually ſwims with its Head under Water, and its Tail above, for fear of being drown'd. A very ſingular Kind of Creature it muſt be own'd; and it is preſum'd a very clean one: As to no other Part of its Body are aſſign'd the Offices which we ſhould readily ſuppoſe were thoſe of the Part mentioned. *Vide Inſpector*, 393.

In this Paſſage our Author, like other great Writers, it muſt be confeſs'd, doth not pay the ſtricteſt Regard to hiſtorical Truth: As the Monſter, here ſpoken of, is not ſaid to be engender'd in *ſmall Beer*; but was the polite Inhabitant of *Kenſington*.

Line 14. *Whilſt thy grim Lion grinds thy Foes to Death.*]

Our

O let my humble Verse, Attention claim;
Nor deem the Friend beneath the Poet's Name.

Blest in thy own *inspectatorial* Stile,
You nobly scorn to hear the Numbers toil,

To

ANNOTATIONS.

Our Author seems to have an Eye to a very curious Piece of History, in the *London Daily Advertiser*, of *January* 8, 1752, which runs thus:

" We hear from the *Bedford Coffee-House* in *Covent-Garden*, " that an unhappy Gentleman of that Neighbourhood, hav- " ing Yesterday Morning in wantonness, thrust his Head in- " to the Mouth of the Lion that resides there, felt the Jaws " unexpectedly close upon him: On this, enquiring with a " hollow Voice, whether he shook his Tail; and, being an- " swered in the Affirmative, he begged the By standers to " pray for him. A terrible Crash was immediately after " heard; and, notwithstanding the uncommon Resistance of " the Skull, it is credibly reported, that the Teeth met " through it. He was immediately after conveyed home, " but his Surgeons are afraid the Wounds will prove mortal." Dr. Hill.

It is not material to consider how much *Wit* or *Truth* is in this Paragraph, if it serves to give the Public a great Idea of the said Lion.

Line 17. *Inspectatorial Stile.*] A manner of writing peculiar to this great Man, which has so often been imitated by

the

To see them fetter'd down to Mood and Tense,
And groan beneath the Infirmity of Sense,

Void

ANNOTATIONS.

the superficial Writers of the present Age; and which our Author seems to speak of as inimitable. The Reader, if any such there be, who is unacquainted with this Stile, will conceive some Idea of it from the following Specimens.——— Speaking of a little Rivulet or Ditch, he says;

"The transluscent Waves coursed one another down the "light Declivity, with an inexpressibly pleasing Variety of "Form, and a confused but very soft Noise of bubbling, "lashing, and murmuring, *among*, *against*, and *along* the "Inequalities and Meanders of its rough Sides, and various "Hollows."

Of a Pond he says,——"The Surface of the Bason was a "polished Plane, unfurrowed by the least Motion, unruffled "by the gentlest Breeze; the setting Sun threw a Glow of "pale Splendor over one Half of it, the rest was silent "Shade."

On Weeds, *&c.* gather'd to one Corner of a Ditch.—— "The fresh Breeze had blown together into this Part of the "watery Expanse, whatever floated *on or near* its Surface." ——How philosophically exact *among*, *against*, and *along*.— *on or near*. At the same Time how poetical and florid! *Transluscent Waves*, *Meanders*, *gentlest Breeze*, *the Glow of Splendor* and *Expanse*. Hence Reader, if thou hast perchance seen only the faint Imitations of this beautiful Stile, thou may'st conceive a more correct Idea of what our Author here so pathetically laments the Want of. Vide *Inspectors* 311, 393, 429.

Void of Politeness, Elegance and Ease.
Ah! what is *Meaning* when compar'd with these!

How then shall I for thee presume to sing,
For thee, borne high on Fame's tenacious Wing,
Lost to thy soft, harmonious, flowing lay,
And curs'd to *mean* whene'er I *sing* or *say*.

Hear then, ye Daughters of immortal Jove!
By the soft Vows of your *Inspector*'s Love,
If not, too jealous of each other's Flame,
You slight the Lover for a Rival's Claim;

Or,

ANNOTATIONS.

Line 24. *Fame's tenacious Wing.*] In this Line appears our Author's commendable Spirit of Modesty in imitating great Men. This Expression being evidently taken from the Motto on the *Lord-Mayor*'s Coach. *Pennâ metuente solvi.* *Vide* State Coach of Sir *Crisp Gascoine*: Also *Horace*'s Ode to *Crisp. Sallust*.

Line 26. *And curs'd to mean whene'er I sing or say.*] Our Author here seems, whether ironically or no, I leave to abler Critics, to complain of a Misfortune which he fears will prevent his Success in Poetry, for no less a Critic and Poet than the great Mr. *Dryden*, says;

He who servilely creeps after Sense
Is safe, but ne'er can reach to Excellence.

Or, if his Gallantry superior charms,
And all the Nine, in concert, fill his Arms,
Like his familiar *Daphnes* here below,
Blessing at once the Poet and the Beau;
Hear and support me in your Fav'rite's Cause,
Inspire my Song, and crown me with Applause.

I sing dire Faction and the cruel Strife
Of Bards that live, and Bards that write for Life;

Of

ANNOTATIONS.

Line 38. *Of Bards that live, and Bards that write for Life.*] I am appriz'd that this Line may be taken in a varied Sense.——Some may imagine, that by a Man's *writing for Life* is intended his writing for a *Livelihood*; and that by Bards that *live*, are meant those who live *independent* of writing; as it is expressed by this Line.

These live to write, and those must write to live.

A kind of Distinction which seems to have been handed down from that immortal Philosopher, Lord Chancellor *Bacon*; who is said to have complained to King *James* the First, lest he should be reduced to *study* to *live*, rather than *live* to *study*. I cannot, however, think this our Author's Drift; but that by *writing for Life*, he meant, *writing as hard as one can drive*, and that he had in his Eye, that Part of the old Ballad of the *Wife of Bath*,

When Adam *heard her say these Words,*
He ran away for Life.

In

Of Fidlers, Coxcombs, Harlequins and Play'rs,
Physicians, Parsons, Fools, and dancing Bears.

Im-

ANNOTATIONS.

In which Case, as *Adam*, according to the Tradition, is in Paradise, or Heaven, he could not be suppos'ed to run to preserve his Life; so that it is clear our Author intended only to convey the Eagerness of the Pursuit of those Bards, who, had the Measure allow'd, he might have said,

Write AWAY *for Life.*

Line 40. *Dancing Bears.*] The Reader is not to take this Expression literally, or think the Poet celebrates real, *four legg'd Bears*; or that he had any View to the famous *Ursi domestici mirabili*, that yielded the *Inspector* an Opportunity of being so very witty last Summer, or to those gentle Bruins that now expose themselves by dancing Hornpipes in the Streets. It is plain he intends no more by the Word *Bear*, than as Sir ALEXANDER DRAWCANSIR has defin'd that Appellation, in his compleat Modern Glossary.

Bear, a Country Gentleman, or any Creature on TWO *Legs that does not make a good Bow.*

COVENT-GARDEN JOURNAL, No. 4.

Neither doth our Author proceed only on *Precedent*, having also philosophical Authority. For *Carolus Linnæus Suecus*, whom I must own I have never read,

" The first of natural Philosophers, as the World with
" Justice stiles him, and as he calls himself *Dioscorides Secun-*

" *dus*

Immortal *Dulneſs*, honour'd on her Throne,
Beheld her Empire ſpreading o'er the Town;
Deſpis'd the Vacuum of her ancient Home,
Where whiſtling Winds pierc'd thro' the hollow Dome;
Forſook the *tatter'd Enſigns of Rag-Fair*,
And ſeiz'd th' unfiniſh'd *Manſion* of the *Mayor*.
Here flock'd her Sons, the ſleepy, blind, and dull,
Each vacant Brain and ev'ry ſolid Skull:

Repeated

ANNOTATIONS.

" *dus* in his *Syſtema Naturæ*, declares, that the Man and " Bear differ only as two Species of the ſame Genus. He " eſtabliſhes in that Work one of his Genera, under the " Name of *Anthropomorphæ*, that is, Creatures having the " human Form, and comprehends under it the *Bear*, the " *Man*, and the *Monkey*."

HILL.

Line 45. *Tatter'd Enſigns of Rag-fair.*] See *Pope's Dunciad*; on which the *Mythology* and *Machinery* of this Poem is, in a good Degree, founded.

Line 46. *Unfiniſh'd Manſion of the May'r.*] The Manſion-houſe.——It is not very clear, whether our Author intended here a Satire on the Imperfection and ill Deſign of that Building, or the ſlow Progreſs made in its Erection; but very probably both.

Repeated *Io*'s their full Joy expreſs'd,
And on the Tables ſmoak'd a City-Feaſt.
Shrieves, Wardens, Aldermen, their Brothers greet,
And each Broad-Bottom ſhook its trembling Seat:
Ev'n thicker Cuſtards did the Cooks afford:
More ſolid Puddings reek'd upon the Board.

The loving Mother then addreſs'd her Sons;
O Children! dear as Birth-day Odes or Puns!
Happy! thrice happy! am I thus to ſee
Your fond Attachment to yourſelves and me:
Nor ſhall I e'er ungratefully forget,
You ſcorn'd to make your *Chamberlain* a *Wit*.
No *Genius* here degrades your ſolemn Meeting.
Right! what has Wit or Senſe to do with eating!

O! ſtill

ANNOTATIONS.

Line 60, *Chamberlain, a Wit.*] On the Reſignation of Sir Sir *John Boſworth*, late Chamberlain of the City of *London*. Mr. *Glover*, whoſe diſtinguiſh'd Merit as a Gentleman, a Merchant, and a Scholar, might have juſtly entitled him to a much higher Poſt of Honour and Truſt, could not obtain the Succeſſion of that important Office.—I have heard ſome Critics condemn this Line as a forç'd Tranſpoſition.—I have, however, no Authority to alter it.

O! still be zealous to support my Laws,
And share my Blessings in the good old Cause.

The Goddess spoke, and strait her opiate shed,
And eke her potent Quintessence of Lead:
All felt its Pow'r, from Marshal to the Mayor:
A double Portion fell to *As*——*l*'s Share.
Then, in the Chair of State, she took her Throne,
And all unanimous the Goddess crown.

Long

ANNOTATIONS.

Line 64. *Good old Cause.*] A Term made use of in almost all Cases, and by all Parties; —— thus a Rebellion, and a Restoration, and the opposite to both, have been honoured with the same happy and significant Phrase.

SCHOLIAST.

Line 67. *Marshal to the Mayor.*] The City-Marshal, an inferior Office so called; and not the Name of a worthy Personage, as may be suspected.

Line 68. *A double Portion fell to* A——l's *Share.*] Sir *C. A.* Knt. and A——n. At present remarkable for a very prudent Resentment subsisting between him and *Crisp Gascoine*, a Gentleman, who honours every other Title he possesses; before the Time of whose Mayoralty commences the *Æra* of this Poem.

Long live Queen Dulness, hoot her darling Owls,
Long live Queen Dulness, shout her fav'rite Fools.

When now behold, in glitt'ring Pomp, ascend
A sister Queen, a Goddess, and a Friend.

Immortal *Pertness*, sprung from *Chaos* old,
Inconstant, active, giddy, light, and bold,
Restless and fickle as her rumbling Sire,
Blind as her Mother, *Night*, could well desire.

Wrought by some Pow'r divine, in equal Pride,
Her Throne ascended by her Sister's Side.

Where hunted Ducks traverse the muddy Stream,
And Dogs initiate their Whelps to swim,
Monsters and Fools assemble once a Year,
And juggling *Hymen* celebrates May-fair,
This Goddess dwelt. Just rais'd above the Ground,
Her Palace varnish'd Silver deck'd around.

Here

ANNOTATIONS.

Line 75, 76.] See *Popo's* Dunciad.

Line 86. *Her Palace varnish'd silver deck'd around*.] *May-fair Wells*, beautified in the manner of most Theatres with lacker'd

Here stood her Merc'ry, here she nurs'd her Apes; 87
Here Magpies chatter'd in a hundred Shapes;
Jackdaws and Parrots join'd th' unmeaning Noise
Of Templars, Coxcombs, Prigs, and 'Prentice Boys.
Far, hence, the Goddess spread her Kingdom wide,
To *Dulness*, as in Birth, in Pow'r ally'd,
She, from her native *Grub-street* to *Rag-fair*,
South to the *Mint* and West to *Temple-bar*,

Included

ANNOTATIONS.

lacker'd Silver, to represent Gold;——a Place resorted to by Clerks and 'Prentices, to perform what they call private Plays to as many of their Acquaintance as they can crowd in, who come to laugh, and in their Turns to be laughed at. It was here Doctor *Hill*, in his younger Days, amused himself in the Science of *Spouting*. A Science ridiculed by one of their own Bards, in an Epilogue spoken at the *Haymarket*.

Nor is our Art to House or Home confin'd,
We rave i'th' Streets, and bellow to the Wind.
Stentor *roar'd out one Day, down* Drury-Lane,
I'll call thee, Father, HAMLET, Royal Dane.
A Porter, *blest with Impudence and Ease,*
Cried, you be damn'd, Sir, call me what you please.

Line 87. *Here stood her Merc'ry, here she nurs'd her Apes.*
HERE STOOD HER OPIUM, HERE SHE NURS'D HER OWLS.

DUNCIAD.

Included ev'ry garrison'd Retreat;
Bedlam, *Crane-court*, the *Counters* and the *Fleet*.
Her Sister boasted as extensive Sway,
Fierce *Broughton*'s bruising Sons her Pow'r obey,
St. *Giles*'s, *George*'s, and the famous Train
Of *Bedford*, *Bow-street*, and of *Drury-lane*;
Ev'n to the licens'd Park her Chiefs resort,
And seize the Priv'ledge of great *George*'s Court.

Lo, *Dulness* now, half-rising from her Throne,
Behold, my Sons, the Part'ner of my Crown;
Let my lov'd Sister equal Honours share,
Pertness, immortal Regent of *May-fair*!

She said. The kindred Goddess all confess'd,
And equal Honours crown'd each royal Guest.

Their

ANNOTATIONS.

Line 99. St. *Giles*'s, *George*'s, &c.] I am somewhat at a Loss to conceive why our Poet should join the Sons of St. *Giles*'s; with the decent, well-dressed Critics of *George*'s, and the *Bedford*. It is true they may be supposed equally pert, but I imagine our Author has a much deeper Meaning. I therefore recommend this Passage to the Critics, hoping they will give some Hints to the Printer, against another Edition of this Work.

Their guardian Virtues in due Order ſtood,
Calm *Prudence*, *Temp'rance*, and ſtern *Fortitude*;
Poetic Juſtice held her Scale between,
And lean'd, by turns, the Beam to either Queen.
Now living Merc'ry Opium out-weighs;
Now ſolid Pudding kicks up empty Praiſe.

The Crowd, below, each varied Impulſe felt.
Part roar and ſing, and Part in Slumbers melt;
Grave Dons and ſkipping Coxcombs fill the Hall,
Theſe ſnore aloud, and thoſe ſtrike up the *Ball*.

At length the Tumult of the Night is o'er.
The Dozers ſleep, the Fiddles ſqueak no more!
The Morning-dawn o'ertakes the *quick* and *dead*;
And home the mighty Drunk are borne or led;
To Buſineſs theſe, to Pleaſure thoſe betake.
Theſe born to hoard a *Plumb*, and thoſe to rake.

Thus bear the ſiſter Queens united Sway;
And *pert*, and *dull*, their ſev'ral Pow'rs obey;

Al-

ANNOTATIONS.

Lines 109, 110.] See *Pope*'s Dunciad.

Line 124.] *Theſe born to hoard a Plumb.*] A *Plumb* means here, the full Sum of twenty thouſand Pounds.

Alternate Honours nod on either Plume,
And both by turns Pre'eminence aſſume.
Hence as one Blockhead ſunk at *Greſham* College,
Another roſe, of diff'rent Taſte and Knowledge.
As lov'd of *Pertneſs* was her dear *Rom-ne*,
As lov'd of *Dulneſs* is her own *Cock—ne.*
So when one Tutor *Cæſar's* Heir forſook,
Another Tutor read another Book.

Now from their Throne they view'd their Empire
round,
Where ſkim the *Shallow*, plunge the vaſt *Profound*,
In dancing Lyrics ſkip the ſcribbling Train,
Or plod in the lame, blank, laborious, heavy Strain:
Saw Journaliſts leave Journals in the Lurch;
Others revive the Science of the *Birch*,

True

ANNOTATIONS.

Line 131. *Dear R——ne.*] A reverend Gentleman, who, being honour'd with the Profeſſorſhip of Aſtronomy at *Greſham* College, attempted in his public Lectures to ridicule the *Newtonian* Philoſophy, and bring that Contempt on the Science which very juſtly fell on himſelf.

Line 132. *Own Coc—ne.*] Succeſſor to the aforementioned Gentleman, who will leave the Science and his Hearers exactly where he found 'em.

True ſcribbling Pedagogues uſurp the Laſh,
And give, like *Bayes*'s Thunder, Daſh for Daſh;
They ſaw *Guildhall* and *Weſtminſter* agree;
At both brow-beating *C——l* earn his Fee;
Smooth-ſpoken *L——d* with ev'ry Witneſs trudge,
And the ſleek *Council* ſpoilt into a *Judge*:
Saw the ſlow Biſhop, with expounding Drawl,
Leave poor St. *James* to graſp a richer *Paul*,

Right

ANNOTATIONS.

Line 144. *Brow-beating C——l.*] I can't think the Mention of this Gentleman here, ſhews any great Diſapprobation; as our Author confeſſes he *earns* his Fee, which is an Encomium our Pleaders at the Bar, in general, don't deſerve.

Line 145. *Smooth-ſpoken L—d, with ev'ry Witneſs trudge.*] Sir *R. L—d*, alluding to the manner of this Gentleman's pleading, which is, in general, with great Mildneſs intermixed with ſarcaſtical Smiles. His *trudging after Witneſſes* alludes to his ſumming up the Evidence, and his frequent Repetition of *I am inſtructed to ſay.*

Line 146. *And the ſleek Council ſpoil'd into a Judge.*] Juſtice *D——n*, eſteem'd an able adviſing Counſellor, which Station it ſeems our Author thought better became him than his later Dignity.

Line 147. *Saw the ſlow Biſhop with expounding Drawl, &c.*] Dr. *S—r*, L. B. of *O—d*, of a ſlow Delivery in the Pulpit.——He left the Rectory of St. *J—s*, where he uſed

to

Right Orthodox, maintains thoſe equal Sinners,
Who ſlight his Sermons, or refuſe him Dinners:
Saw *Newgate*'s Ordinary chatter on as faſt,
As if each Sermon was to be *his* laſt;
Degreeleſs Doctors, regular-bred Quacks,
In Merc'ry and in Opium all go Snacks:
Saw the *choice Spirits* noiſy Vigils keep,
And ſing their drunken Brethren faſt aſleep:

Block-

ANNOTATIONS.

to expound during the Winter, for the Deanery of St. *P—l*'s. ——He took great Offence at a certain Alderman in his Mayoralty, before whom he preached, becauſe his Lordſhip did not invite him to Dinner.

Line 151. *Newgate's Ordinary chatter on.*] The Contraſt between theſe two Divines is very high;—the Prelate addreſſing the moſt polite Audiences in Terms ſo homely, that he *who runs may read*, and ſo ſlowly, that he who crawls may keep up with him;—the *Ordinary* telling the moſt ignorant of all Wretches, that *Death is an opake Body, that eclipſes the Brightneſs of Eternity*, with all the Volubility of a School-boy.

Line 155. *Saw the choice Spirits noiſy Vigils keep.*] A kind of modern Bacchanalians, who diſtinguiſh themſelves by frequent, nocturnal Meetings; called by ſeveral Names, ſuch as *Comus's Court*, *Britiſh Carnival*, *High Borlace*, &c.——The Scene is a Mixture of ſinging, drinking, blaſphemy, and Noiſe, as at the ancient Feaſts of *Bacchus*, among the

Heathens,

Blockheads and *Bloods* in Pit and Boxes roar,
Support a Pantomime and damn a *Moore*;
Arraign the Traitor *Garrick*'s Insolence,
Who dar'd to satirize the Want of Sense,

To

ANNOTATIONS.

Heathens, and very deserving the Satire of a Christian Poet. ——Their Priests are dignified with the Title of *Stars*, and their High-Priests by *Stars* of the *first Magnitude*; so that it is plain in what Esteem this *Pagan* Worship is held. *O tempora! O mores!* And yet the Bishops, and the Parliament, take no Notice of these Things, as if they were not.

J. Westley. *vivâ voce.*

What Mr. *Westley* remarks is undoubtedly very just, that the Clergy and the Parliament should look into these outrageous Proceedings. But what will that reverend Divine say when I assure him, that not only Members of that high Court, but even Brothers of his own sacred Function, are themselves *Bacchanalians*?

Line 158. *Damn a Moore.*] Mr. *Moore*, a Poet of great Modesty and Merit, both as a Gentleman and a Writer. His last Comedy, called Gil Blas, met with very unjust Treatment on the Stage; for, notwithstanding it had many Faults, as he himself allows, the best Critic would not have condemned the Taste of the Town, for giving it more Applause than they have bestowed on many less-deserving Pieces.—— His *Female Fables* are Master-pieces of good Sense and Elegance.

To join with *Popery* and *France*, at once,
In *Powder-Plot*, to blow up ev'ry Dunce:
And leagu'd, to rob each free-born *English* Skull,
Of *Right* and *Priviledge* of being *dull.*
Saw Students, Play'rs and Taylors, Casuists nice,
Discuss vague Metaphysics in a trice:
Part *Woolston*, *Bolingbroke* and *Annet* foil,
And hold, unread, *Le Clerc*, *Van Dale* and *Moyle*,
In lukewarm *Middleton* find out a Flaw,
Staunch to the *Text* and *Kennedy* and *Law*,

Plain

ANNOTATIONS.

Line 167. *Annet foil.*] A Writer, who has published many Pieces after the manner of *Woolston*, particularly about the *Trial of the Witnesses*,—a virulent Opposer of the Christian System.——He is now concerned in a periodical Pamphlet, called the *Free Correspondent*.

Line 170. *Kennedy and Law.*] Two of the most singular and incomprehensible Writers the World ever produced. Mr. *Kennedy* has wrote an astronomical Treatise deduced from the *Pentateuch*, in which he prefers the *Ptolemaic* System as next to that of *Moses*, and gives Sir *Isaac Newton*, *Copernicus*, *Tycho Brahe*, and all the rest to the Devil.——He says, *The* Newtonian *Astronomer truckles to the Suggestions of the* Delphean *Tripod, and suffers himself to be juggled into an artificial Computation, by the Ambiguities of a Dæmon.*—A rare Fellow! Mr. *Law* is his Equal, for he confesses he has not

his

Plain as a Pike-ſtaff make the Diff'rence clear,
Between a Knight o'th' Poſt and Knight o'th' Shire:
Others with *Locke* and *Newton* Truths diſpute,
Still blunder on, and ſtill themſelves confute,
Eſtrang'd as much from Reaſon as from God,
Miſtake *Ontologos*, and kiſs the Rod;
Aim at the Mark of Science, blindly wiſe,
So fire plump Buff-coats when they ſhut their Eyes,

Root

ANNOTATIONS.

his Light from Reaſon, nor writes to reaſon; he is indeed a ſeraphic Writer, and may poſſibly write for celeſtial Beings, for no Man can underſtand him.

Line 176. *Miſtake Ontologos.*] The Name prefixed to a Pamphlet, which made ſome Noiſe laſt Winter, and was called, *An Eſſay to prove the Soul of Man is not, neither can it be, immortal.* This Piece, tho' intended as a Satire on the ſceptical Reaſoning in vogue, and purpoſely ſtuffed with threadbare Arguments, and worn-out Propoſitions, was ſwallowed by the Deiſts, who laviſhed Encomiums on its Author, 'till he vouchſafed to undeceive them by publiſhing as weak a Reply in the ſame Name, meerly to convince them how little he was in earneſt. It was attacked, however, from the Pulpit on all Sides, except from Mr. Orator *Henley*, who delivered an Elogium on its Author, remarking at the ſame Time, that he had not advanced his ſtrongeſt Arguments, for which, however, his Sagacity being at fault, he could not account.

Root up Religion, cancel *Good* and *Evil*,
At *Butcher-Row*, the *Queen's-Arms*, or the *Devil.*

They

ANNOTATIONS.

Line 180. *At Butcher-Row, the Queen's Arms, or the Devil.*] Places where a Company of People meet together to dispute on the several Topics of Religion, Government, Trade, *&c.* Every Person, in his Turn, having the Liberty of speaking a stated Time, as much, or as little to the Purpose as he pleases.——Sir *Alexander Drawcansir* has fallen under a gross Mistake, in supposing the former of these Societies to have subsisted some Ages ago; which, considering his Account is so just, in other Respects, is a little surprising. It is true he might be led into this Error, from the many absurd Opinions and obsolete Expressions they make use of; but certain it is, it has not existed many Years, and doth still exist,——the Fragments he has got *verbatim* are, however, really curious, one of which I cannot help inserting here.

The Debate whether Religion was of use to Society.

——A worthy Member on this Occasion got up, and spoke thus.

" I Ham of Upinion, that Relidgin can be of no youse to
" any mortal Sole; bycause as why, Relidgin is no youse
" to Trayd; and if Relidgin be of no youse to Trayd, how
" ist yousefool to Sosyaty. Now nobody can deny, but that
" a Man maye kary on his Trayd very wel without Relid-
" gin; nay, and beter two, for then he may wurk won

" Day

They ſaw their Bards and Critics all appear:
Dull *Rolt*, long-ſteep'd in *Sedgeley's* nut-brown Beer:

Kenrick,

ANNOTATIONS.

" Day in a Wik mor than at preſent; whereof nobody can " ſaye but the ſeven is mor than ſix: Beſides, if we haf no " Relidgin we ſhall have no *Pairſuns*, and that will be a " grate Savin to the Soſyaty; and it is a *Makſum* in Trayd, " that a Peny ſaved is a Peny got."

COVENT-GARDEN JOURNAL, No. 8.

Line 182. *Dull Rolt, long ſteep'd in* Sedgely'*s nut-brown Beer.*] Mr. *Rolt*, Author of the *Weſtminſter* Journal, in which our Author, in the ſame Sentence with Mr. *Fielding*, had been treated with Abuſe: Likewiſe of ſeveral Poems and Pamphlets now forgotten, ſuch as the *Roſciad, Cambria*, the *Theatrical Conteſt, A Reply to Mr.* Fielding'*s Diſcourſe on Robberies, a Monody on the Death of the Prince*, and *the Goſſip's Chronicle in the Old Woman's Magazine.* Our Author, with much Juſtice, has joined in the ſame Line *Ben Sedgely*, of *Temple-Bar*, ſometimes the Father of Mr. *Rolt*'s Pieces, and who is very proud of being eſteemed an Author, placing himſelf much higher than his Predeceſſor *Ward*, a Publican celebrated in the *Dunciad*, tho' not poſſeſſed of even half his Talents. *Ben* being really a very dull Fellow, and remarkable for nothing but emptying a Tankard.

ANON.

Kenrick, whose sing-song Verse the Ladies chuse;
More honour'd by his Wenches than his Muse:

Derrick

ANNOTATIONS.

Line 183. *Kenrick.*] A very young Poet, and a Pretender to almost all kinds of Writing.——It is the Misfortune of this Youth, that, unless he finishes what he goes about in a Day or two, the World never see it afterwards. He published a Monody on the Death of the late Prince, dedicated to the Countess of *Middlesex.*——His anonymous Pieces are numerous, and on various Subjects. He wrote the two Essays on the Immortality of the Soul, concerning which, see Note on Line 174. Also many other Disquisitions for the Exercise of his Pen, and to amuse the Dabblers in Argument.——His *Old Woman's Dunciad* is an extraordinary Instance of that Impetuosity of Genius, which, tho' redounding little to his Honour, is very offensive to his Adversaries.——Mr. *Smart* having advertised an *Old Woman's Dunciad*, and given out that this Writer would share the Benefit of his Satire, he immediately wrote that Piece, and published it under the same Title. After which Mr. *Smart* never prosecuted his Design of publishing his Poem.——He is also the Author of innumerable poetical, philosophical, and political Pieces, dispersed up and down in the News-Papers and Magazines. It is no Wonder, however, he should be so indefatigable a Writer, as he is perhaps the only one that never takes any Pains.

Derrick made fine with *Gentleman*'s lac'd Coat,
Ah! wherefore soil'd by *Murphy*'s cruel Foot!
Jones who intends to live at *Colley*'s Death,
So waits the good old *Laureat*'s parting Breath;

Has

ANNOTATIONS.

Line 185. DERRICK *made fine with* GENTLEMAN'*s lac'd Coat.*] Mr. *Derrick* and Mr. *Gentleman*, both Players and Poets. The former, Author of the *Dramatic Censor*, a very *modest* Work, in which the Errors and Inaccuracies of all our best Poets were to be pointed out: The latter, Author of *Sejanus*, a Tragedy, never acted; *Fortune*, a Rhapsody, and some other Pieces; particularly *Osman*, a Tragedy, in Manuscript.

Line 186. *By* Murphy'*s cruel Foot.*] *An Irishman that has kick'd me*, says Mr. *Derrick*. It seems this Gentleman, who sometimes amuses himself with the Pen, thinking Mr. *D.* unworthy his Resentment, as an Author, disciplin'd him in a manner a little too rough for his Constitution.

Line 187. *Jones, who designs,* &c.] a Poet, who addressed the Earl of *C——d*, when Lord-Lieutenant of *Ireland*, in a Copy of Verses, which obtained him the Favour of that Nobleman, who brought him over to *England*. He publish-ed here a Poem on seeing the late Prince of *Wales*'s Picture, of which the Publick took little Notice. A Tragedy also of this Gentleman's, called, *The Earl of Essex*, has been long expected on the Stage.

Has made his *Threnody*, 'gainſt Fate ſhall end him;
'Cauſe *Cibber* to the *Bayes* did recommend him:
Tho' here the *Laureat*'s Policy is known:
Worſe Odes the better will ſet off his own:
Macklin religious, *Henderſon* polite,
Woodward, *The. Cibber*, and the Mimes that write:
With theſe, droll *Howard*, and laborious *Shiells*
With Mobs of *Boys* and *Parſons* at their Heels:

Saw

ANNOTATIONS.

Line 190. *To the Bayes did recommend him.*] Mr. *Cibber*, in a late Illneſs, wrote a Letter warmly recommending him to the Laurel, expecting hourly his own Diſſolution, which Epiſtle the honourable Perſonage, to whom it was addreſſed, eſteemed, as it really was, a remarkable Inſtance of the Laureat's Greatneſs of Mind and extraordinary Merit.

Line 193. *Macklin religious*, &c.] Mr. *Macklin*, a famous Player, and Author, particularly celebrated for his Harangues on religious Subjects, at the Oratory of the *Robin-Hood*.

Line 193. *Henderſon polite.*] Author of an Hiſtory of the late Rebellion in *Scotland*, and a Tragedy never acted.

Line 195. *Droll* Howard.] *Harry Howard*, an Author and Humouriſt, well known at the Routs and Aſſemblies of *Old-Street* and *Broad St. Giles's*.

Line 195. *Laborious* Shiells.] Author of the *Daily Gazetteer*; ſome Time ago, Amanuenſis to Mr. *Johnſon*. He is alſo Author of *Marriage*, a poetical Eſſay, and many other

anony-

Saw *O——y*, without Excuſe for Bread,
Rake up the ſacred Aſhes of the Dead,
Traduce the Mem'ry of his once-lov'd Friend,
And brand the honour'd Name he ſhould defend:
Saw ſcribbling Stationers, and link'd with thoſe,
The Sons of Novel and poetic Proſe;
Long-winded *Richardſon*, with *Sm-llet* join'd,
D——y and *Crockat* puffing in the Wind;
With ſlattern Females traipſing up and down,
Searching Adventures, to amuſe the Town:
Saw puerile *Harvey* on a Cock-horſe ride;

With

ANNOTATIONS.

anonymous Pieces; alſo a great Orator at the *Butcher-Row.*

Line 197. Lord C--r--y's Life of *Swift.*

Line 203. *Sm--llet join'd.*] Author of *Roderick Random, Peregrine Pickle,* the *Regicide,* a Tragedy, and ſeveral Tranſlations.

Line 204. *D——y* and *Crockat.*] Mr. *D——y,* Author of ſeveral dramatic Pieces. A Man of ſome Ingenuity, but more lucky in his Deſigns, than able to execute them. *W--r--r--n, vivâ voce.*

Line 207. *Saw puerile* Harvey *on a Cock-horſe ride.*] Mr. *Harvey,* Author of Meditations and Contemplations, a very *florid* Piece.

With *Gibbons*, *Boyce*, and fifty more beſide
The bawdy-ſcribbling *Knight*, the preaching *Lord*,
And what the Stews, the Shops, and Stalls afford.

All theſe the Siſter Queens, with Joy confeſs'd,
For lo! their Eſſence glow'd in ev'ry Breaſt!
But *Pertneſs* ſaw her Form diſtinctly ſhine
In none, Immortal *Hill*, ſo full as thine.
Drinking thy Morning Chocolate in Bed,
She ſaw thy *Daphne*'s Neck ſupport thy Head,
Saw thee ſlip on thy Night-gown and retire
To muſe profoundly by thy Parlour Fire:
By turns thy Slippers dangling on thy Toes;
Slippers that never were diſgrac'd from Shoes!
Saw where thy Learning, in huge Volumes ſtood,
Part letter'd Sheep, Part gilt and painted Wood;
Where thy lov'd *Antients* in Diſorder lay,
Daily perus'd, *for Mottos for the Day*;

Thy

ANNOTATIONS.

Line 208. *Gibbons and Boyce.*] Mr. *Gibbons*, by ſome called a ſecond Dr. *Watts*. See his *Juvenilia*.

Boyce, a ſecond Duck, according to the *Inſpector*. He has wrote a Comedy, a ſtrange Piece.

Thy *Ovid*, *Horace*, and thy *fav'rite Tully*,
Thy *Ainſworth*, *Bailey*, and thy well-thumb'd *Lilly*.
Saw where thy Maggots, in whole Myriads, riſe,
Or in thy Brain, or in thy dear Dirt-pies.

When

ANNOTATIONS.

Line 225. *Thy* Ainſworth, Bailey, *and thy well-thumb'd* Lilly.] It will ſeem ſomething ſtrange, that our Author ſhould join theſe Moderns ſo unluckily with the Ancients; as it is impoſſible he ſhould himſelf be ſo ignorant; and very unlikely the learned Perſonage he addreſſes ſhould know no better; ſince he himſelf remarks on illiterate Scribblers. " We ſhall ſee the modern Eſſayiſt, who has hardly Gram-" mar enough to arrive at Concord, larding every other " ſentence with ſome Tranſcript, from an Author it is im-" poſſible he ſhould have read, not becauſe it is neceſſary, " but becauſe it is *Greek*, for what he has been ſaying in " *Engliſh*."

It is true, a certain writer, who pretended to take off, or copy the Doctor's Writings exactly, did quote *Lilly*, and ſupaum'd the Paſſage upon *Virgil*; but it is impoſſible to ſuppoſe an Author, who could cenſure others in the manner above-quoted, ſhould be guilty of ſuch Forgery.

SCHOLIAST.

Line 227. *Dear Dirt-pies.*] Dirt-pies, the Preparations for engendering Animalculæ.

When thus the Goddess of *May-Fair* bespoke
Her royal Sister. Gentle Sister, look,
See where my Son, who gratefully repays
Whate'er I lavish'd on his younger Days.
Whom still my Arm protects to brave the Town,
Secure from *Fielding*, *Machiavel*, or *Brown*;

Whom

ANNOTATIONS.

Line 234. *Machiavel, or Brown.*] Our Author seems here to hint at the Plot carried on last Summer at *Ranelagh*, in which Mr. *Brown* was the principal Person concerned.—— Hear the Account of the Diligence used in detecting the Contrivers.

" Warrants were issued out on *Wednesday* Night from " Mr. Justice *Lediard*, and early on *Thursday* Morning from " the Right Honourable the Lord-Mayor, for apprehending " all the Persons concerned with Mr. *Brown* in the Assault " upon Dr. *Hill*, on *Wednesday* Night in the Passage at *Ra-* " *nelagh*. The Officers have been ever since in search after " them, but none of them are yet taken. Yesterday, at " Noon, the *Marshals* of the *Lord-Mayor* entered the Cham- " bers which some Gentleman had lent to *Brown* in the " Temple: But he escaped the Search, by concealing him- " self in a Coal-hole: About ten last Night he was seen to " go out muffled up in a Great-coat, and with a Handker- " chief tied over his Face. Notice was immediately sent to " the City, and the proper Officers are posted to wait his

" Return.

Whom Rage nor Sword e'er mortally ſhall hurt.
Chief of an hundred Chiefs o'er all the *Pert!*

Reſcu'd

ANNOTATIONS.

" Return. The Servants of the Chambers, while he lay in " the Coal-hole, pretended he had early made his Eſcape, " and was by that Time far enough out of Reach. Such " Meaſures are now taken, that it will not be eaſy either " for him, or any of the reſt to get off, unleſs they have " already anticipated the Sentence of the Law by a volun- " tary Baniſhment. It would be well if the Police of *Paris* " were imitated here, and Accounts were taken of thoſe who " make the Appearance, or ſomething which they intend " ſhall be like the Appearance of Gentlemen, with no vi- " ſible Way of living." *H--ll.*

There were ſome People, however, who, knowing the Conſequence of this illuſtrious Perſonage, imagined the Scheme for depriving this Kingdom of his Pen and Services, much deeper laid than was generally thought, and that, notwithſtanding the trivial Pretence of a private Quarrel, the Politicians of the *French* King's Cabinet were no Strangers to the Proceſs of this Plot. This will appear very plauſible, if we reflect how, on a particular Occaſion, the great Mr. *Dennis* was diſturbed by a *French* Privateer, hovering about the Coaſt of *Suſſex*, in order to take him for writing a Pamphlet againſt the Intereſt of that Court. How the Doctor was offended at his Chriſtian Majeſty, or whether it be not out of Envy to this Kingdom itſelf, that this Plot was laid againſt its Inſpector-General, I can't determine.

SCHOLIAST.

Rescu'd an Orphan Babe from *Common-Sense*,
I gave his Mother's Milk to *Confidence*;
She, with her own *Ambrosia*, bronz'd his Face,
And chang'd his Skin to monumental Brass:
This *Shame* or *Wit*, successless, shall oppose,
Unless, so will the Fates, they seize his Nose.
This luckless Part the young *Achilles* lick'd,
And tho' he cannot blush, he may be kick'd:
Yet still his Pen provokes the Fates' Decree,
In Scandal dipt, and elemental Tea;
Still he rails on, and, when attack'd, replies,
Recants his own, and blabs his Neighbour's Lies;

Or,

ANNOTATIONS.

Line 248. *Recants his own, and blabs his Neighbours Lies.*] It is most surprizing the Incredulity of Mankind, that the Word of anonymous Authors should be taken before a Man's own Hand-writing. Dr. *H—* is accused of being a great Liar, nay, this Opinion has so far prevailed, that his own Acknowledgment of finding himself in an Error, has been thus censured in an Epigram.

What H--ll *one Day says, he the next does deny,*
And candidly tells you,—'tis all a damn'd Lie:
Dear Doctor,—this Candour from you is not wanted;
For why shou'd you own it?—'tis taken for granted.

Now

Or, guiltleſs of Deſign, as Madmen fight,
Falls foul on Friends or Foes, or wrong or right;
Humane to ſpare when forc'd himſelf to run,
As *G-pe* once ſav'd the grateful Mother's Son.

Such

ANNOTATIONS.

Now the Doctor himſelf ſays, *There is no Vice ſo univerſally deteſted as falſehood*, and takes for the Motto of his Paper, *Juvenal's Confeſſion. I know not how to tell a Lie.*——Surely, ſurely, thoſe who thus accuſe the Doctor muſt be miſtaken, or the Doctor muſt ſtrangely miſtake his own Talents and Abilities.

SCHOLIAST.

Line 251. *Humane to ſpare*, &c.] It is certainly the moſt convenient thing in Life to make a Virtue of Neceſſity, and conclude, when it is out of our Power to revenge, *there is not any thing ſo virtuous, as to forgive an Injury.*

INSPECTOR, No. 553.

Line 252. *As C--pe preſerv'd the grateful Mother's Son.*] A grave Lady of the Order of Mendicants, craving Charity of General *C--pe*, to excite his Liberality, pleaded her Gratitude for Favours received, and poured Bleſſings on him for being the Preſerver of her Son's Life. On which the General had Curioſity enough to enquire who her Son was, and how he could be inſtrumental in ſaving his Life.—Ah! God bleſs your Honour, returned ſhe, *when you ran away at* Preſton-Pans, *my Boy ran after you, or he would certainly have been killed.*

EDINBURGH TOWN-TALK.

Such is his Pen, and ſuch this Son of mine,
Then ſhed thy Opium, and adopt him thine;
Let him exalted o'er our Empire reign,
From *Shepherd's-Market* e'en to *Roſemary-lane:*
Tibbald dethron'd, thy *Dunciad* Reign is o'er,
Thy *Gildon*, and thy *Toland*, are no more.

Thus ſpoke the Queen, and pauſing for Reply,
Her Siſter roll'd her broad, lack-luſtre Eye,
And thus return'd. O *Pertneſs!* Goddeſs! Queen!
With whoſe my Reign has e'er conſiſtent been,
O had thy Thought anticipated mine!
So witneſs *Jove* I honour thy Deſign!
My Opium then had fill'd his ſhallow Skull,
And all the *pert* had bow'd with all the *dull.*
But ſee my darling Son, whom I have choſen,
Chief of my Chiefs among an *hundred Dozen*,
With Cyder muddled, or inſpir'd with Bub,
In *Newb'ry*'s Garret, or in *Henly*'s Tub,
With Coachmen, Coblers, and ſuch dainty Folks,
For Mugs of Porter, pun and crack his Jokes;
In ſacred Verſe, at my own *Cambridge* riſe,
Write by himſelf and bear from *all* the Prize;
As oft *poor Jack* his Brother Wit hath done,
Ran for a Wager with himſelf, and won:

For

For him the regal Sceptre I design,
As worthy thy distinguish'd Love as mine.
Me, he confess'd, tho' nurs'd by *Common Sense*,
Tho' *Wit* and *Genius* held him in Suspense,
Thy *Hill*, from Gratitude, obeys thy Laws,
My *Smart*, from Love and Rev'rence to our Cause:
Yet, that due Merit meet its due Renown,
That he who best deserves may wear the Crown,
Nor these our darling Chiefs, from partial Care,
The highest Honours of our Empire share,
Let all our Sons, in Emulation, rise;
And he who most atchieves shall claim the Victor's
Prize.

Line 282. *My Smart*, &c.] Mr. *Smart*, a Person of real and great Genius.

INSPECTOR, No. 350.

It is true, Mr. *Inspector* gives another Account in some succeeding Papers of this real and great Genius, concerning which, see Notes on our second Book.

THE END.

www.ingramcontent.com/pod-product-compliance
Lightning Source LLC
Chambersburg PA
CBHW020231030726
47497CB00009B/3048
* 9 7 8 3 3 3 7 4 0 9 9 4 4 *